Marc paused, overwhelmed by what he had to tell her.

Ellie rose and opened the sideboard. She poured two whiskies. Large ones.

'I don't drink this except in emergencies,' she told him. 'I suspect I need it now. Maybe we both do. So tell me.'

He took the glass and drained it, and then he looked at Ellie. He could still see the girl he'd loved behind those tired eyes. He could still see the laughter, the fun... But he could also see the care and the responsibility.

He watched her shoulders brace yet again, and he hated it.

'Ellie, I'm now Crown Prince of Falkenstein and Felix is my son. It takes a year to formalise a divorce in Australia, so Felix was born while we were still legally married. This may mess with all our lives in ways I can't imagine, but once I'm crowned Felix will take my current title. Your son—*our* son—will be the new Crown Prince of Falkenstein.'

Dear Reader,

What *is* it with royalty? The combination of tradition, power and wealth is a heady mix that I suspect would be difficult to handle in real life, but as a writer I love playing with 'what ifs?'. What if an entire royal family was wiped out in one hit? That's a theme that's been explored before—an unimaginable tragedy, but to a fiction writer the idea's gold. What if the unexpected heir to the throne is a doctor, dedicated to his calling, who wants nothing to do with royalty? And what if, years ago, that doctor had a secret son, who's suddenly the new Crown Prince?

The situation had me wiggling my toes in the sand in delight as I took my dog for her daily beach walk. I love a good 'what if?', and if it combines the pageantry of a royal coronation, a feel-good romance and a secret baby thrown in for good measure— hooray! The dog and I needed to walk our legs off in order for me to sort out all the complications, but we loved how it all turned out. At least I did. Sadly, Bonnie was too busy chasing seagulls to care.

Marion

REUNITED
WITH HER
SURGEON PRINCE

BY
MARION LENNOX

Published in Great Britain 2017
By Mills & Boon, an imprint of HarperCollins*Publishers*
1 London Bridge Street, London, SE1 9GF

ISBN: 978-0-263-06998-3

Printed and bound in Great Britain
by CPI Antony Rowe, Chippenham, Wiltshire

Marion Lennox has written over one hundred romance novels, and is published in over one hundred countries and thirty languages. Her international awards include the prestigious RITA® Award (twice) and the *RT Book Reviews* Career Achievement Award for 'a body of work which makes us laugh and teaches us about love'. Marion adores her family, her kayak, her dog, and lying on the beach with a book someone else has written. Heaven!

Visit the Author Profile page
at millsandboon.co.uk for more titles.

CHAPTER ONE

THE BRAND-NEW Crown Prince of Falkenstein managed three hours of nightmare-filled sleep. He rose at dawn, desperate for coffee and a walk to clear his head. Instead, he found the Secretary of State waiting. The massive palace dining table was covered with newspapers, and their front pages all screamed versions of the same.

Entire Royal Family Killed in Plane Tragedy!

'This is what you get for breaking rules,' Josef said in greeting, and Marc wanted to thump him. At such a time, to be thinking of rules...

He headed for the huge silver coffee pot before deigning to answer. Being Crown Prince had to count for something. Half a cup of coffee in, his head was clear enough to respond. 'How did breaking the rules cause this?'

'Heirs in succession to the throne should never travel in the same plane,' Josef told him. 'Your uncle and his wife, your cousin, his sons and their assorted mistresses. All in the one small plane, on one indulgent holiday—and at vast expense when so much needs to be done at home. No consideration for rules. It's all part of the same. Your grandfather was a warlord. Your uncle was a playboy. Your cousin was a wastrel, and his sons were already mixing with women of the worst kind.' Josef heaved a sigh and laid the newspaper aside. 'Now it's up to you, boy, to fix the mess.'

'I have messes of my own to fix.'

'Not as big as this one. Your Highness—'

'Don't call me that.'

'It's who you are,' Josef said simply. 'You're Marc Pierre Henri de Falken, Crown Prince of Falkenstein. After your coronation you'll be His Majesty.' He hesitated but then forged on. 'And, might I say, this tragedy is appalling, but for the country it may well be a force for good.'

'I'm no prince,' Marc exploded. 'I'm a surgeon and I need to stay a surgeon. If you look at the mess our country's health system is in...'

'That's why you have no choice but to take the throne.' There'd been hours now to take in the news, and the country's chief administrator obviously saw the path ahead as being without obstacles. 'You've been doing your best with rundown hospitals, fighting for funds from a royal family who doesn't care. Now the reins are yours. Think of the bigger picture. The schools. The courts. Our welfare system. If you refuse the throne then it goes to Ranald de Bougier, and heaven help us if that happens. He'll propel us back to war.'

'But I don't want it.'

Marc took his coffee and stood at the vast bay window of the King's private dining room. Though it was the informal part of the palace, even this part was intimidating.

Marc's father had been the ignored younger son of the King. He'd been a pacifist who had hated his father's warlike tendencies. He'd studied medicine, he'd struggled to build the country's health system and he'd been appalled when the King propelled the country into a meaningless border conflict.

Marc had only been in this palace once, as an awed seven-year-old, brought to be introduced to a family his parents had little to do with. There'd been continual fights about health funding and then an epic fight when war broke out. Marc had never been back. Until now.

Marc raked his long surgeon's fingers through his dark hair and stared into the future with horror.

He glanced through to the family's 'informal' sitting room. It was an opulent display of gilt, brocades and priceless furniture.

He wanted nothing to do with it.

The huge mirror above the dining room's massive fireplace showed Marc as he was, a thirty-five-year-old surgeon, a man who was weary from operating until midnight and who'd been brought to the palace straight from Theatre. After four hours of horrified discussion, he'd fallen asleep in his clothes. He was wearing faded jeans and a plain white T-shirt. He hadn't had time to shave.

A king? *Ha!*

'I can't,' he said simply. 'I love my work.'

'You have no choice,' Josef told him, and Marc thought of the mess the country's healthcare system was in, of the theatres without equipment, of the rundown hospitals, of the endless waiting lists.

If he turned his back on the throne, he could do more of what he was doing now. He could save lives, one patient at a time. If he accepted the throne...how many more could he save?

Josef was right. He had no choice, but he felt ill. He dug his hands into his pockets and kicked the heirloom rug at his feet.

'We need to move on,' Josef was saying, gently now, obviously knowing his argument had been won. 'You need to face the press. We need to get you shaved, dressed in something...' he eyed Marc's clothes with distaste '...more fitting. And we need to have a statement ready. The country's in uproar. We need reassurance of continuity. Even at this time we need the implication that this tragedy might make things better.'

'Why? Surely there's no need to talk of the future yet?'

'There is a need,' Josef told him. 'The country's desperate for a lifeline. You know there's no one fit to form government. Marc, we need steadiness and the promise of a better future. Moving on, we need to find you a wife. Get you a son. I believe you'll make a great king, and your sons after you.'

And that made Marc think of something else. Something that had played on his mind many times these past ten years. Something else that made him unfit to be royal.

He hesitated but it had to be said.

'There may be another...issue.'

'Yes?' Josef looked as if nothing could surprise him, but Marc knew this would.

'I have a son.'

He was right. To say Josef looked stunned would be an understatement.

Marc refilled his coffee mug and realised this was the first time ever that he'd said those words.

I have a son. The words seemed unreal in this situation that was already unreal. Having a son was part of another world. And yet, when it was said out loud it assumed a reality that shocked him as well as Josef.

He watched the colour drain from the old man's face. His grandfather's and then his uncle's reign had been marred by scandal after scandal, Marc knew, and now he was asking Josef to cope with more. He was under no illusions as to the old man's role in the royal household. Somehow Josef had kept the royal family intact, holding the country together. He'd served his country with honour. He didn't deserve to have to cope with this.

'A son...' Josef whispered. 'Where? When?'

'You knew I was married, briefly?'

'I...yes.' The old man was struggling to regroup, sifting long-forgotten information about a Marc he barely knew, a doctor on the outer fringes of the royal family. 'I had heard that,' he said. 'It was just after you qualified as a doctor, wasn't it? In Australia. A momentary aberration. You came home when war broke out. The divorce was almost immediate?'

'It was,' Marc said heavily. 'The marriage was…a mistake. I didn't know Ellie was pregnant when we separated, and the child was born well after I returned. A son.'

'It was never said.'

'There was no need. Neither of us was in a position to keep a child. I was flying back into a war zone. Ellie was a second-year medical student and she wished to continue. The baby was adopted at birth.'

'Formally adopted?'

'Yes.'

'Do you know the adoptive parents?'

'No. I had nothing to do with the adoption.'

He watched Josef think through the ramifications while he considered a third coffee. Josef's background was legal, Marc knew, and he'd spent a lifetime getting the royal family out of trouble. Scotching scandals was his principal skill. Marc could almost see the cogs whirring.

'There should be no concern,' he said at last. 'This was a child conceived in an impulsive marriage when you were little more than a child yourself. If he's been formally adopted, there can be no claim on inheritance. That can be explained to him if there's ever contact. But then…' he hesitated '…there may be more immediate repercussions. As the unexpected heir to the throne, you'll face media scrutiny of the worst kind. The country hardly knows you, so the media frenzy will be extraordinary. They'll dig out this old marriage. Where's your ex-wife now?'

'I presume she's still in Australia. I haven't spoken to her in years.'

'Tell me about her.'

He was too tired for this. He was too tired for everything. To be dredging up memories of Ellie…

But, strangely, it was easy. She should have been a distant memory. Instead she was a vivid reality, a warm, vibrant woman, curvy, laughing...

Except when he'd last seen her, ten years ago, standing in the airport lounge. She'd been wan with what he'd learned later was morning sickness, but she'd been resolute in the direction they had to take.

'We've been stupid, Marc, but you know what we need to do.'

He did. The senseless war was bringing his country to its knees. He was a qualified doctor—just—but his place was at home. Ellie was only two years into her medical course. Even after he'd learned of the pregnancy, they'd both known there was no room in their lives for a child.

'Ellie's a doctor too,' he told Josef but he didn't even know that for sure. Their separation had been absolute. She'd reluctantly allowed him to provide funds to keep studying—because of the pregnancy—but the amount she'd decided was 'over the top' had been returned and he hadn't heard from her since.

'Our marriage was a mistake by both of us,' she'd told him. 'I have no intention of profiting by it.'

And he'd had no choice but to agree. He'd been desperate to be with her for the birth but the conflict at home had escalated. The need for doctors had been dire, and by the time her—their?—baby was born, getting out of the country had been impossible.

Her email telling him of the birth had been business-like, informing him only of the bare fact that she'd given birth to a boy. The feeling he'd had then was indescribable. Pain. Helplessness. Anger at a situation which made it impossible for him to claim his son.

And when he'd finally found a way to phone, her response had been curt.

'Leave it, Marc. He'll have a good home, I promise.

You're needed where you are and so am I. Our marriage was a fantasy, and we need to put it behind us. Good luck, Marc, and goodbye.'

Their son was no longer their son, yet the anger and helplessness had stayed. And guilt. Disconnecting from that phone call had seemed the hardest thing he'd ever done, and there'd been many times since when mother and child had been in his dreams.

'She's intelligent enough to be discreet?' Josef asked, dragging him back to the present.

'Of course.' It was a snap, inappropriately terse.

'Has she married again? Has she told her new husband?'

'I have no idea. She made it clear she wanted no further contact.'

'And the divorce? It was amicable?'

He thought of Ellie's face that last time. They'd both known the impossibility of their situation. There'd been no argument, just bleak acceptance. 'Yes.'

'That's a help.' Josef wasn't seeing Marc's emotion. He was thinking ahead, anticipating trouble. 'But you don't know where the boy is?'

'Ellie never shared adoption details.' He hadn't asked. In the midst of the chaos of war, he hadn't had the energy to ask questions, and it had seemed unfair—even cruel— to question Ellie's judgement.

'Then that's how it must remain,' Josef decreed. 'For the child's sake, it's imperative his adoption records remain confidential. There's no problem with inheritance but the media would love it.'

'I can't guarantee—'

'We need to guarantee,' Josef said flatly. 'If the media finds him, can you imagine the headlines? We need to contact this woman before the media does. Press the need for silence. Pay her if necessary.'

'She won't accept payment.'

He remembered that last conversation almost word for word.

'You have a disaster to deal with. How many people dead, Marc? What's the adoption of one child compared to that? Marc, you've helped enough. I don't want to continue contact. It's over.'

'We'll do what's necessary and do it fast,' Josef was saying. 'If she's remarried and hasn't told her husband, then it could become messy. I'll brief one of our best lawyers. We'll research her background while he's on the way to Australia. He'll meet her face to face, tell her exactly what's involved, tell her she has to keep her mouth shut. Most countries allow contact between adoptive parents and birth mothers. If she has that contact then she needs to be silent about where he is. Did she name you as the father?'

'No.' That was down to him too. She'd asked him in that first curt email:

'Do you want your name on his birth certificate?'

The choice he'd made was wrong.

In his defence, he'd been stressed to the point of breaking. The war had been going badly. He'd been overworked past exhaustion, doing work far beyond his range of expertise, but there'd been no choice. For every patient he'd treated there'd been three more waiting. He'd also been gutted by the thought of Ellie having the baby alone. He couldn't bear the thought of what he'd lost. He'd made an instant decision then that he still regretted.

'Leave it blank,' he'd told her. *'I can't be there for him. I have no right to be his father. The adoptive father should have all the rights.'*

It still hurt but Josef's face cleared. 'There you are, then,' he said. 'Even if the media finds out, it can be implied he wasn't yours. What better reason to end the marriage?'

'That's not fair to Ellie.'

'We'll pay her enough to compensate.'

As if that would work.

He turned and faced out of the window again, across the manicured palace gardens to the mountains in the distance. Somewhere, on the other side of the world, Ellie was making a life for herself, without him and without their son. It was a decision they'd made together.

Ellie was tough. She'd had to be, with her background. She called life as she saw it.

And now? A legal expert would come blustering in from her past, offering her bribes. Even asking her to swear a child wasn't his.

He thought of the Ellie he'd known. She was feisty, opinionated...moral. She also had a temper.

'No,' he told Josef. 'It could turn the situation into a disaster.'

'There's no other way,' Josef told him.

'There is,' he said heavily and he saw his path clear. This part, at least. 'If this is as important as you say, then let me do it. I must be able to fly under the radar for a few days. I'll face the media this morning and then I have a week's grace until the funeral. Say I'm stricken with grief, incommunicado. If I board a plane this morning no one will notice—the media surely won't expect me to be leaving the country. I'll go to Australia and talk to Ellie myself. I'll make sure the child's privacy is protected and there are no cracks the media can chisel open. And then...'

He put down his coffee cup. It was fine china with the royal coat of arms emblazoned on the front, and he found himself thinking almost longingly of the paper cups he grabbed after all-night Theatre shifts. That part of his life was over and he had to accept it. 'Then I'll come home,' he said heavily. 'I'll bury my family and I'll accept the throne.'

CHAPTER TWO

LIFE AS BORRAWONG'S only doctor was sometimes boring, but just as often it was chaotic. If one person went down with the flu, the whole town usually followed. Kids never seemed to fall out of trees on their own. Ellie had a great team at the hospital, though. Usually she could cope.

But not with this.

Two carloads of kids had been drag racing on a minor road with a rail crossing without boom gates. Maybe the drifting fog had hidden the crossing's flashing lights and the sight of the oncoming train until it was too late. Or maybe alcohol had made them decide to race the train. Whatever the reason, the results had been disastrous.

The train had just left the station so it had been travelling slowly, but not slowly enough. It had ploughed into one car, pushing it into the car beside it.

If the train had been up to speed, every occupant of the cars would have been killed. Instead, Ellie had seven kids in various stages of injury, distress and hysteria. Parents, grandparents, aunts, uncles, cousins—practically the whole town—were crammed into the waiting room or spilling into the car park outside.

Air ambulances were on their way from Sydney but the fog was widespread and there were delays. The doctor from the neighbouring town was caught up with an unexpected traumatic birth.

She was the only doctor.

Right now, she was focusing on intubating seventeen-year-old May-Belle Harris. May-Belle was the town's champion netballer, blonde, beautiful, confident. At least she had been. Her facial injuries would take months of reconstruction—if Ellie could get her to live past the next few minutes.

Ellie's team was fighting behind her, nurses and paramedics coping with trauma far beyond their training. But while she fought for May-Belle's life, she had to block them out.

'You can make it,' she told May-Belle as she finally got the tube secure. At least she now had a safe air supply. The girl was deeply anaesthetised. She should have an anaesthetist to watch over her before she could be transferred to Sydney for specialist reconstructive surgery. Instead of which, she had Joe.

'Can you take over?' Ellie asked the seventy-year-old hospital orderly. 'Watch that tube like a hawk and watch those monitors. Any change at all, yell. Loud.'

'Louder than these?' Joe said with a wry grimace. There were six others kids waiting for attention, plus the injuries and bruises of the train crew who'd been thrown about on impact. Some of these kids—the least injured—were... well, loud would be an understatement. One of the girls was having noisy hysterics and the very junior nurse allocated to her couldn't quieten her.

With years of experience, Ellie knew she could quieten her in a minute but she didn't have a minute.

'Grab me by the hair and pull me over here if you need me,' Ellie told Joe. Block everything out and focus on that breathing.

Moving on...

A boy with bubbling breathing also needed urgent attention. There had to be a punctured lung.

A girl with a shattered elbow needed her too. She risked

losing her hand if Ellie didn't re establish a secure blood supply soon. The lung had to be a priority but that elbow was at an appalling angle. If the blood supply cut...

And what if there were internal injuries?

Focus, she told herself. *Do what comes next.*

He was heading for Borrawong's Bush Nursing Hospital.

Marc hadn't been surprised when Josef's discreet investigators had told him Ellie was back working here. This was where her mother had lived, the town Ellie was raised in.

The last time he'd seen her she'd been heading home to care for her mum.

Borrawong was a tiny town miles from anywhere. A wheat train ran through at need, hauling the grain from the giant silos that seemed to make up the bulk of the town. The train felt like the town's only link with civilisation.

He'd never been there. 'As long as Mum stays well, I'm never going back,' Ellie had told him. She was jubilant at having escaped her small-town upbringing, her childhood spent as her mother's carer. Until those last days when their combined worlds had seemed to implode, she'd put Borrawong far behind her.

But now Josef's investigator had given Marc the lowdown on Borrawong as well. 'Population six hundred. Bush nursing hospital, currently staffed with one doctor and four nurses, servicing an extended farming district.'

To be the only doctor in such a remote community, to have returned to Borrawong... What was Ellie doing?

Had her mother died? Why had he never asked?

Because he had no right to know?

He landed in Sydney, then drove for five hours, heading across vast fog-shrouded fields obviously used for cropping. It was mid-afternoon when he arrived, and midwinter. The time difference made him feel weird. The main street of Borrawong—such as it was—seemed deserted.

The general store had a sign: 'Closed' pinned to the door. The town seemed deserted.

Then he turned off the main street towards the hospital—and this was where everybody was.

The tiny brick hospital was surrounded by a sea of cars. There were people milling by the entrance. People were hugging each other, sobbing. Two groups were involved in a yelling match, screaming abuse.

What the…?

He pulled up in the far reaches of the car park and made his way through the mass of people. By the time he reached the hospital entrance, he had the gist. A train had crashed into two carloads of kids.

How many casualties?

The reception area was packed. Here, though, people were quieter. This would be mum and dad territory, the place where the closest relatives waited for news.

He made his way towards the desk and a burly farming type guy blocked his path.

'Can't go any further, mate,' the man told him. 'Doc Ellie says no one goes past this point.'

Ellie. So she was here. Coping with this alone?

'I'm a doctor,' he told him.

The man's shoulders sagged. 'You're kidding me, right? Mate, you're welcome.' He turned back to his huddled wife. 'See, Claire, I told you help'd come.'

He was the help?

There was no one at the reception desk, but double doors led to the room beyond.

A child was sitting across the doors. He was small, maybe nine or ten years old.

He was in a wheelchair but he didn't look like a patient. He was seated as if he was a guard. He had his back to the doors and he held a pair of crutches across his chest. Anyone wanting to get past clearly had to negotiate the crutches, and the kid was holding them as if he knew how to use them.

Right now he seemed the only person with any official role.

'I'm here to see Dr Carson,' Marc told him. The kid's expression was mulish, belligerent. The crutches were raised to chest height, held widthways across the doors. 'I understand there's been an accident,' Marc said hurriedly. 'I might be able to help.'

'No one goes in,' the kid told him. 'Unless you're Doc Brandon from Cowrang, or from the air ambulance. But you're not.'

'I'm a doctor.'

'You're not a relative? They all want to go in.'

'I'm not family. I'm a doctor,' he repeated. 'And I might be able to help.'

'A real doctor?'

'Yes. I'm a surgeon.'

'You have a funny accent.'

'I'm a surgeon with a funny accent, yes, but I do know how to treat people after car accidents. I knew Dr Carson back when we were both training. When she was at university. Believe me, if she needs help then she'll be pleased to see me.'

Pleased? That was stretching it, he thought grimly, but right now didn't seem the time for niceties.

The crutches were still raised. The kid was taking a couple of moments to think about it. He eyed him up and down, assessing, and for a moment Marc took the time to assess back.

And then...

Then he almost forgot to breathe.

The kid was small and skinny, freckled, with dark hair that spiked into an odd little cowlick. He was dressed in jogging pants and an oversized red and black football jumper. One foot was encased in a worn and filthy trainer. The other foot was hidden by a cast, starting at the thigh.

He could be anyone's kid.

His hair was jet-black, his brows were thick and black as well, and his eyes...they were almost black too.

And those freckles! He'd seen those freckles before, and the boy's chin jutted upward in a way Marc remembered.

He looked like Ellie. But Ellie had glossy auburn hair that curled into a riot. Ellie had green eyes.

The kid had Marc's hair and Marc's eyes.

Surely not.

And then, from the other side of the door, someone screamed. It was a scream Marc recognised from years of working as a trauma surgeon. It spoke of unbearable pain. It spoke of a medical team without the resources to prevent such pain.

Shock or not, now wasn't the time to be looking at a kid with dark eyes and asking questions.

'You need to let me in,' he told the boy, urgently now, as he pulled himself together. 'Ask Dr Carson if she needs help.'

'You really are a proper doctor?' The boy's voice was incredulous.

'I am.'

'Then go on in.' There was suddenly no hesitation. He peeped a grin at Marc and there was that jolt again. He knew that grin! 'But you're either in or out,' he warned. 'If another doctor ever walks into this town Mum says we'll set up roadblocks to stop them leaving. That's me. I'm the roadblock. No one gets past these crutches.'

'Ellie!'

Chris was Ellie's best trained nurse. While Ellie was treating the kid with a suspected pneumothorax she'd put Chris in charge of the girl with the smashed elbow. Lisa

Harley had smashed a few other things as well, but it was her elbow that was Ellie's greatest concern. The fracture was compound. She'd found a pulse on the other side of the break but it was faint. The blood supply was compromised.

But the kid with the pneumothorax had taken priority.

'I've lost the pulse,' Chris called urgently. 'And I'm worrying about her blood pressure. Ellie…'

She couldn't go. She had to release pressure in the chest of the kid under her hands. One lung had collapsed—she was sure of it. Any more pressure and she'd lose him.

A life or a hand…

'Five minutes,' she called back to Chris. Could she close this in time? No matter. She had to focus on what she was doing.

The door swung open.

It was too soon to expect the air ambulance from Sydney. It was too soon to expect the doctor from the neighbouring town, but Felix wouldn't have let anyone in unless they could help. Unless they were a doctor.

So she looked up with hope—and then felt herself freeze.

Marc.

He was older. There was a trace of silver in his jet-black hair. He looked taller, broader…more distinguished.

But he was still Marc.

Marc, here!

Her world seemed to wobble. If she'd had time she would have found a chair and sat down hard.

The boy she was treating needed all her attention. A smashed rib piercing the lung meant air was going in and not getting out. The pressure would be building. The second lung could collapse at any minute. She needed to insert a tube to drain the air compressing the lung and she needed to do it fast.

Marc was here.

'Where can I help?' he asked and somehow she forced her world back into focus. No matter why he was here; the one thing she knew was that he was a skilled doctor. A surgeon. Every complication that had suddenly hit her world had to give way to imperative.

'Chris needs help,' she told him, gesturing towards the nurse. 'Lisa Harley, seventeen, smashed elbow—I'm sure it's comminuted. There must be fragments of bone cutting the circulation. Feeble pulse in her fingers until a moment ago, but now nothing. Chris says blood pressure's dropping too, but I haven't had time to figure out why. I've given her morphine, ten milligrams. She probably also has alcohol on board.'

Marc's attention switched instantly to Lisa, lying wanly on the trolley. The morphine had kicked in but the kid looked pallid.

'I'm on it,' Marc said, in his perfect English with that French-plus-something-exotic accent that had made Ellie's toes curl all those years ago. He crossed to Lisa and touched her fingers. He'd be feeling for the pulse, Ellie knew. Even though it was Marc, she could only feel relief.

'You're right,' he said calmly, smiling down at Lisa in a way that would be medicine all by itself. 'Hi, Lisa. I'm Dr Falken. We need to get your arm sorted, but it's your lucky day. I treat hurt elbows all the time.' He checked her blood pressure and frowned. 'We might also check your tummy and see if there's anything else going on.' He flicked a glance back to Ellie. 'Lisa's priority one?'

'I'm coping with a pneumothorax but I have it under control,' she told him. She hoped. 'We also have a severe facial injury but I've intubated and she seems stable. Nothing else seems life-threatening. Chris, can you assist Marc? Everyone, this is Dr Marc Falken. He's…he's an old friend from university and he's good. Give him all the assistance he needs. Marc, sorry, but you're on your own.'

* * *

There was no time for shock or questions. There was only time to work.

With Chris's help he did a fast X-ray. The elbow was a jigsaw of shattered bone fragments.

It wasn't the greatest of her problems, though. Lisa's blood pressure continued to drop. Chris helped him set up an ultrasound and that confirmed his fears.

Ruptured spleen. She'd have internal bleeding. This was life or death.

Ellie had far more than she could cope with already. This was his call.

He'd like a full theatre of trained staff. He had Chris.

But, even though Chris looked as if she could be anyone's mum, the nurse was cool, efficient and exactly what he needed.

'I can give an anaesthetic,' she told him. 'I've done it before when Ellie's been in trouble. We can take Lisa into Theatre and go for it if that's what you want.'

He'd worked on battlefields with less help than this. 'That's what I want.'

From the next cubicle, Ellie must have heard. She was focusing on the kid with the punctured lung but she must have the whole room under broader surveillance.

'You can't just straighten for the time being?' she called.

Marc moved so he could talk without being overheard. The last thing Lisa needed to hear was a fearful diagnosis. 'There are bone fragments everywhere,' Marc told her. 'I can re-establish blood supply but if something moves it'll block again. It's not safe to transfer her without surgery. But priority's the ruptured spleen. I'll need to go in to check for sure but her blood pressure's dropping fast and the symptoms fit.'

She swore. 'You can do it?'

'I can.' His gaze swept the room, seeing the mass of

trouble she was facing. 'You have enough on your hands.'
More than enough.

'I can't help,' she said.

'I know.'

'Then do it. Chris, give him all the help he needs.'

And Chris was already wheeling Lisa's trolley through
the doors marked Theatre.

He had no choice but to follow.

The cavalry arrived two hours later. Helicopters with
skilled paramedics. The doctor from the neighbouring
town. Everyone and everything she needed was suddenly
there, and Ellie was able to step back and catch her breath.

The door to Theatre was still closed. There hadn't been
time to investigate. She'd had to trust that Marc knew what
he was doing.

Now, though, as paramedics fired questions at her, as
each of these kids got the attention they needed, she was
able to think of what—and who—was behind those doors.

'I have a kid with a shattered elbow and possible ruptured spleen,' she told the senior paramedic. 'A visiting
surgeon was on hand. He's in Theatre now.'

'Here?' the guy said incredulously, and Ellie thought
again of the mixed emotions his arrival meant for her.

Marc was behind those doors. Her old life was a life of
secrets. A life that now had to be faced.

She took a deep breath and opened the door to Theatre.

Chris was at the head of the table. She smiled and gave
Ellie a swift thumbs-up, then went back to monitor-gazing.

Chris was magnificent, Ellie thought, not for the first
time. Ellie had needed to talk her charge nurse through
an anaesthetic more times than she could count and she'd
coped magnificently every time. She should be a doctor
herself. She practically was.

But her attention wasn't on Chris.

Masked and gowned, Marc could be any surgeon in any

theatre anywhere in the world. He was totally focused on the job at hand.

'Nearly closed,' he growled and his voice was a shock all by itself.

She'd never thought she'd hear it again.

'What's happening?' she asked.

'We've stabilised the elbow, removing bone fragments that could shift. The circulation should hold until she receives specialist orthopaedic attention. The worst risk was the spleen. It was a mess. There was no choice but removal. Sorry, Ellie, to leave you with everything else. I had Chris slip out and tell Joe to call if there was any priority you couldn't cope with, but then we went for it.'

'He's done the whole thing,' Chris breathed. 'He's removed the spleen but he's done so much more. He's stopped the internal bleeding completely. Blood pressure's already rising. And the elbow! Look at the X-rays, Ellie. To get the circulation back. He's saved her life and he's saved her arm. Oh, Ellie, I can't tell you...'

'Thanks to Chris,' Marc growled, still focused. 'You have a gem of a nurse, Ellie.'

'Don't I know it,' she said a trifle unsteadily.

This was surgery way beyond her field of expertise. Maybe she could have diagnosed and removed the spleen but the pneumothorax had been just as urgent. She would have lost one of the two kids, and how appalling a choice would that have been? But the elbow... She glanced at the X-ray, saw the mess, and knew without a doubt that Lisa would be facing amputation if Marc hadn't been here.

Marc's battlefield training had come to the fore. She never could have done this alone.

A bullet had been dodged. Or multiple bullets. She wanted to sit down. Badly.

It wasn't going to happen.

'I'm just applying an external fixator and then I'm done,' Marc told her. 'Ten minutes? I gather the air ambulance is here. I'd like Lisa transferred to Sydney as soon as possible. The elbow will need attention from a specialist. I'm not an orthopod.'

'You could have fooled me,' Chris muttered, and Ellie looked at Marc and thought, *What good fairy brought you here today?*

And then she thought of the repercussions of him being here and she stopped thinking of good fairies.

She didn't have time to go there. She had to face the relatives.

But there was no longer any urgency. She had room for thought.

Marc was here.

Good fairies? She didn't think so.

The first chopper took the most seriously injured, including Lisa, but the boy with the pneumothorax left by road. Air travel wasn't recommended when lungs were compromised. The road ambulance also took the driver of one of the cars and his girlfriend. The pair had suffered lacerations; the girl had a minor fracture. They could have stayed, but feelings were running high in the town and a driver with only minor injuries could well turn into a scapegoat.

The second chopper, a big one, had places to spare and the battered train crew chose to leave on it. They, too, could have been cared for here, but their homes, their families, were in Sydney. Borrawong Hospital was suddenly almost deserted.

But Marc was still inside and, as Ellie watched the second chopper disappear, that fact seemed more terrifying than a room full of casualties.

'You can get through this.' She said it to herself, but she was suddenly thinking of all the times she'd said it before. During the trauma of being the kid of a defiant, erratic single mum with cystic fibrosis. The roller coaster of a childhood living with her mother's illness. The relief of her mother's first lung transplant and then the despair when it had failed.

And then the moment the doors had closed at Sydney Airport and Marc was gone for ever. The moment she'd looked at the lines on the pregnancy testing kit. The moment she'd seen her baby's ultrasound.

The day she'd made the decision to keep her baby, to stay here, to cope alone.

But it was no use thinking of that now.

The sun was sinking behind the town's wheat silos, casting shadows that almost reached the hospital. Somewhere a dog was barking. This was Borrawong's nightlife. Marc was about to see Borrawong at its best.

Why was he here?

'You can get through this,' she said again but heaven only knew the effort it cost her to turn and re-enter the hospital.

Felix was still in the waiting room. He'd pushed his wheelchair behind the reception desk and was engrossed in a computer game but he looked up as she entered and grinned.

'Got rid of them all?'

'We have. Felix, you were wonderful.'

'I know,' he said, his grin broadening. 'I kept 'em all out. Except the doctor with the funny accent. He's still in there now, helping clean up. Joe says if we have a doctor who cleans we should lock the doors and keep him. He said he's your friend?'

'I...yes. He's someone I knew a long time ago. When I was at university.'

And Felix's face changed.

Uh oh.

Felix was smart. He was also right at the age where he was asking questions, and the questions had been getting harder.

'So you met my dad when you were at uni. Why won't

*you tell me his name? The kids at school reckon he must
have been married to someone else. Or he was a scumbag.
Otherwise you'd tell me. Why can't I meet him?'*

And now Felix had met a strange doctor three hours
ago while he'd been bored and had time to think—a guy
who'd appeared from the past, a man his mum had never
talked about.

A man with hair and eyes exactly the same as his.

'Is he my father?' Felix demanded and Ellie closed her
eyes.

And when she opened them Marc was in the doorway.

He'd ditched his theatre gear. He was wearing casual
chinos and a white open-necked shirt.

His dark hair, wavy just like her son's, was rumpled.
He'd raked it, she thought. He always raked his hair.

Felix looked like him. Felix was Marc in miniature—
except for the freckles. And the wheelchair.

But there was no use denying it. Felix's face was bris-
tling with suspicion, but also with something else. Hope,
perhaps? He wanted a father.

How wrong had it been not to tell Marc what she'd done?

She glanced at Marc again. His face was impassive.
Shuttered.

She thought of the first time she'd met him. She'd been
nineteen, a second-year university student, working her
butt off to put herself through medicine. Marc had been
twenty-four, just completed training, headed to Australia
for a gap year before he started surgical training.

He'd intended working his way around Australia's coast-
line, but in his first week in Sydney there'd been an international conference on vascular surgery. He'd cadged an
invitation because, gap year or not, he was interested.

She'd been there as a waitress. On the edges. Soaking
up knowledge any way she could. She'd been working the
crowd, carrying drinks.

An eminent vascular surgeon had been holding forth

to a small group of similarly esteemed professionals, talking of the latest cardiovascular techniques. She'd paused to listen, intrigued by the discussion of a technique she'd never heard of.

And then one of the group had caught her eye, maybe suspecting she was eavesdropping. *Uh oh.* If she lost this job it'd be a disaster. She'd spun away fast—and crashed into Marc.

Her tray had been loaded with red and white wine and orange juice. The whole lot had spilled down his front. Glasses smashed on the floor. The attention of the whole room had suddenly been on her, and she'd stood, appalled, expecting to be sacked.

But Marc had moved with a decisiveness that had taken her breath away. He'd stopped people moving onto the broken glass, and he'd talked to her boss before she could say a word.

'I'm so sorry,' he'd said in his lovely broken English. 'So stupid. I was caught by something Professor Kramer was discussing, and it seemed important to catch it. So I turned suddenly and I hit your waitress hard. *Mam'selle*, are you hurt? A thousand apologies. Sir, may I make recompense? The cost of the glasses? The wine? Something extra for your work? And, *mam'selle*, I will pay the cost of your cleaning...'

He'd charmed her right back into her job—and that night, when she'd finished work, he'd been waiting for her at the staff entrance.

'I messed with your night,' he said simply. 'The least I can do is take you to supper.'

'It was my fault.'

'The fault is immaterial. It was my body you crashed into. Therefore my body will propel you to supper.'

He'd been irresistible. His looks, his accent, his smile... His kindness.

She'd fallen in love right there and then and, amazingly, he'd seemed to feel the same.

And now he was here.

'Ellie?' he said gently, but there was no smile.

He was waiting for an answer.

Felix was waiting for an answer.

She looked from one to the other. Her son. Her ex-husband. The man she'd loved with all her heart.

Once. Not now.

Is he my father?

There was nowhere to go.

'Felix, this is Marc Falken,' she managed and was amazed at the way her voice sounded. It was almost steady. 'He's from Falkenstein, near Austria, in Europe. Marc's a doctor. He and I met at university and for a few short months we were married. But then there was a war in Marc's country, a disaster that lasted for years. He was needed. I'd imagine he's still needed. But, for whatever reason, he's here now, and yes, Felix, Marc is your father.'

CHAPTER THREE

After that, the night seemed to pass out of her control. Felix was excited and full of questions. Marc seemed calm, courteous and kind.

She could stay silent—and she did.

Between Marc and Felix, they sorted that Marc would have dinner with them. The hospital cook was making bulk fish and chips, so they ended up at the kitchen table in Ellie's hospital apartment with a mound of fish and chips in front of them.

Ellie simply went along with it. She didn't have the strength for anything else.

She ate her fish and chips in silence and was vaguely grateful for them—how long since she'd eaten?

There was a bottle of wine in the fridge. She offered it to Marc but he refused. 'Jet lag,' he told her and she nodded and reflected that that was how she herself was feeling. She was pretty much ready to fall over now.

And Marc? He must be shocked to the core, but he was being kind.

For Felix was hammering him with questions. One part of Ellie was numb, but there was still a part of her that was taking in Marc's responses.

'Are you really a surgeon?'

'Yes.'

'Do you work in a big hospital?'

'I travel a lot, Felix. I'm in charge of the country's health system. I do operate when I'm needed, but a lot of my time's spent checking our remote hospitals are up to standard.'

'What's remote? Like the Outback here?'

'We don't have deserts,' he told him. 'But we do have mountains. Lots of mountains and many of our tiny hospitals are cut off in bad weather. Like your mum's hospital here, they're a long way from anywhere and it's my job to see they're not cut off completely.'

'But you still operate.'

'I love my job so yes, I operate, whenever I can. I have an apartment in one of the city hospitals and I operate there when I'm needed.'

'Like this afternoon.'

'Like this afternoon.'

And then the questions got personal.

'Are you married?'

'No.' He glanced at Ellie and Ellie concentrated fiercely on her pile of chips.

'Why not?'

'I guess I've been too busy.'

'You weren't too busy to marry my mum.'

'I wasn't,' he said gravely. 'But your mum and I were both students then, so we had more time. We hadn't realised just how many responsibilities we faced. There was a war in my country and I had to go home. Your grandmother was ill and your mum was needed here. There wasn't time for us to stay married.'

And finally Felix fixed his eyes on his father and asked the question she'd been dreading. 'There was time to make me,' he said flatly. 'Didn't you want me?'

If ever she wanted to turn into a puddle of nothing, it was now. What had she been thinking, not telling Marc what she intended?

It had been for all the right reasons, she told herself, but her silent reasoning sounded hysterical. It sounded wrong.

And Marc? He'd respond with anger, she thought, and he had every right. He could slam her decision of nine years ago. He could drive a wedge between her and her son, give Felix a reason to turn to her with bewilderment and betrayal.

Marc glanced at her, for just a moment. Their eyes locked.

She saw anger, but underneath there was mostly confusion. And concern.

All that she could see at a glance. Why?

Because she knew this man. She'd married him. Three glorious months...

'Felix, this takes some understanding,' Marc said, and whatever betrayal he was feeling seemed to have been set aside.

But she hadn't betrayed Marc, she told herself. She'd told him the truth.

Sort of.

'Your mum and I were very young when we met,' Marc continued. 'We were not much more than kids. We fell in love and we got married. It was all very fast and very romantic. But sometimes you do things that you hope might work out, even if they probably won't. Have you ever done that?'

'Like riding Sam Thomas's brother's bike down the hill at top speed,' Felix said. Marc was talking to him as an adult and he was responding in kind. 'It was too big for me and I couldn't make the brakes work but there was a grassy paddock at the bottom so I sort of hoped it'd be okay.'

'It wasn't, huh?'

'No,' Felix said but he peeped a cautious smile at Marc, obviously looking for a reaction. 'I broke my leg. Getting married was like that? Getting on a bike with no brakes?'

'I guess so,' Marc said and Ellie saw a faint smile in response. 'Only in this case we didn't break our legs. A war started in my country. A big one. There were many, many people killed and more hurt. And your grandma was ill here. So your mum and I had to part.'

'You didn't write to me.'

'No,' Marc said softly and Ellie thought, *Here it comes.* But it didn't.

'I didn't write,' Marc continued. 'And I'm very, very sorry.'

And, just like that, he'd let her off the hook. Of all the things he could have said, the anger, the blame...

He could be telling Felix it was his mother's fault, his mother's deception. Instead of which, he was simply apologising.

'When I left I didn't know your mother was pregnant,' Marc said. 'And when she told me, I was in the middle of a war zone, helping people survive. But I should have come back for you and I'm very sorry I didn't.'

All the questions Felix had been firing at her had been becoming increasingly belligerent. Increasingly angry.

She'd known that she'd have to face that anger some time. Now, Marc had taken it all on himself. He'd let her off the hook.

She'd been staring into her water glass sightlessly, numbly. Now she looked up and met his gaze.

Not quite. She wasn't off the hook. There were still questions she had to answer. Accusations to face.

But not from her son. For that, at least, she was so grateful she could weep.

'So, the wheelchair,' Marc said, and she thought, *He hasn't asked it until now.* That was a gift in itself. For most people it was the obvious focus, and now he asked. 'What's the matter with your leg?' And it was a simple follow-up on the preceding conversation. 'That was the bike, huh? Bad break?'

Felix hated the questions. The sympathy. The constant probing from a small community. 'How are the feet? Does it hurt? Oh, you poor little boy...'

Felix routinely reacted either by pretending he hadn't heard or by an angry brush-off. Now, though, for some reason he faced the question head-on.

'I was born with club feet,' he told Marc. 'Talipes equinovarus. You know about it?'

'I do,' Marc told him. 'Rotten luck. Both feet?'

'Yeah, but the left's worse than the right. I had to have operations and wear braces for years and now the right one's almost normal. But my left leg won't stay in position and it's been shorter than the right one. Then I broke it and the surgeon in Sydney said let's go for it and see if we can get a really good cure for the foot as well as for my leg. So it was a big operation and I'm in a wheelchair for another two weeks and then braces again for a bit. But Mum reckons it should be the last thing. Won't it, Mum?'

'We hope so.' Ellie was having trouble getting her voice to work. Somehow she had to make things normal.

As if they could ever be normal again.

She had to try, but she had a moment's grace. It was well past Felix's bedtime. 'You have school in the morning,' she managed. 'Bed.'

'You weren't at school today?' Marc asked.

'The doctor who did my leg had a clinic at Wollongong,' Felix told him. 'Mum and I drove down early and got the first appointment. We only just got back when the accident happened.'

'Which is why you need to go to bed now,' Ellie said, struggling to sound firm.

'But you'll stay?' Felix looked anxiously at Marc. 'You'll be here when I get home from school tomorrow?'

'I'm booked into the motel.'

'So you will be here.'

Marc met her gaze and held it. Questions were asked in that look. Questions she had no hope of answering.

But obviously Marc was more in charge of the situation than she was. He knew what he was here for, even if she didn't.

'Yes, Felix, I will.'

'Cool,' Felix told him. 'I might bring my mate to meet you. He's always ragging me about not having a dad. You want to meet him?'

'Of course.'

'Cool,' Felix said again and yawned.

'You did a great job today, by the way,' Marc told him and Ellie found herself flushing. *You compliment my kid, you compliment me.* It shouldn't happen like that but it did. And then Marc added, 'Both of you.'

'You didn't do too badly yourself,' Ellie muttered. She could feel herself blushing but there wasn't a thing she could do about it. 'Are you heading back to the motel now?'

'In a while,' Marc told her. 'You and I need to talk.'

'Felix and I usually read. His leg often aches and reading helps him sleep.'

'Would you mind if I read to my son tonight?'

And what was she to say to that?

My son.

Her world had changed.

Felix was obviously exhausted, too tired to ask any more questions but, under instructions, Marc sat on his bed and read. This wasn't a storybook, though. What he and Ellie were obviously halfway through was a manual on the inner workings of the Baby Austin—a British car built between nineteen-twenty-two and nineteen-thirty-nine.

The back axles of spiral bevel type with ratios between 4.4.1 and 4.6.1 5.6:1. A short torque tube runs forward from the differential housing to a bearing and bracket on the rear axle cross member...

It was enough to put anyone to sleep, Marc thought, but as he read Felix snuggled down in his bedclothes and his eyes turned dreamy.

'One day I'm going to find one and do her up,' he whispered. 'Do you know anything about cars?'

'A bit. I don't know much about short torque tubes.'

'But you could find out about them with me,' Felix whispered. 'Wouldn't that be cool?'

And then his eyes closed and he was asleep.

For a few moments Marc didn't move. He sat looking down at the sleeping child.

He had a son.

A kid who coped with club feet with courage. A kid who guarded doors with crutches. A kid who wanted to introduce his dad to his mate and who needed help with something called short torque tubes.

A son to be proud of.

The feeling was almost overwhelming.

He'd known of Felix's existence for years but it had always seemed theoretical rather than real. He hadn't been with Ellie when she'd found out she was pregnant. He hadn't been here for the birth.

He hadn't questioned her decision to put the baby up for adoption.

Maybe he should feel anger that she'd kept this from him for so long but all he managed was sadness. It had been an appalling time. His country had had to come first, but what a price he'd paid. He'd missed out on nine years of Felix's life.

Walking away from Ellie had been the hardest thing he'd ever had to do in his life. He'd felt it had broken something inside that could never be repaired. And when she'd told him she was pregnant, and he couldn't go to her...

The nights he'd lain awake on his hard bunk and thought of her; the fantasies he'd had of his dream life, where they could be a family...

But the dreams had been just that. Fantasies. He hadn't been able to go to her. He'd been in no position to be a husband or a father.

He'd lost his family. He'd lost Ellie.

He thought of her now, out in the sparse little sitting room she called home. She'd changed after work, into faded jeans and an old windcheater. She looked tired. Worn.

He'd thought he'd had to cope with trauma. How much more had she had to deal with?

Felix was deeply asleep. He touched his son's face, tracing the cheekbones. His son who looked like him. But who also looked like Ellie.

Back in the kitchen, Ellie was waiting for him. She'd cleared the dishes and was standing with her back to the sink, hands behind her back. She looked...trapped.

'Marc, I'm sorry,' she managed. 'I should have told you that I kept him.'

'Why didn't you?' He wasn't sure where to go with this. There were accusations everywhere.

'You didn't want him.' But she shook her head. 'No. That's unfair to you. At the time, neither of us wanted him. We were kids. The pregnancy was a mistake, Marc, as was our marriage. We should have known that it was never going to work. Our backgrounds were so different it was impossible.'

'If it hadn't been for the war...'

'And if it hadn't been for my mum's illness...' She shrugged. 'But even without, there were responsibilities. You never told me how important your role was at home. And maybe I didn't tell you how much my mum needed me.'

'So when did you decide to keep him?'

She tilted her chin, like a kid facing the headmaster. Defiant.

'I came back here after you left,' she told him. 'As I told you I had to. Mum's lung transplant had failed. She loved the freedom the transplant gave her, the illusion of health, but she didn't take care. She refused to follow the doctors' instructions and maybe I can understand why. For the first time in her life she felt healthy and she made the most of it. Until she crashed. Then, you knew I had to put my studies on hold to care for her. When I found I was pregnant, life became even more impossible.'

He remembered. He'd received the email after a day coping with massive trauma wounds, when he was so exhausted the words had blurred.

Ellie was pregnant.

What could he do? Where he was, he couldn't even phone her.

But the email had been blessedly practical. She couldn't support a baby and care for her mother. She still—eventually—wanted to study medicine. There were so many good parents out there desperate for a baby, she told him, so the logical answer was surely adoption. Did he agree?

He'd felt gutted but there seemed no choice but to accept her decision. The war looked as if it would drag on for years. Ellie would have to cope on her own, so what right did he have to interfere?

'So I was back here and pregnant,' she told him. 'Mum was totally dependent. I had your funds which kept us, but there was no way I could go back to university. University, our marriage, they seemed like a dream that had happened to someone else. Mum seemed to be dying and the pregnancy hardly mattered. When I thought about the pregnancy at all, it was just a blanket decision that adoption was the only answer.

'Then, when I was thirty weeks pregnant, Mum was so bad she had to be hospitalised. And one of the nurses asked if I was looking after myself—if I'd had my checkups, my scans. It was the first time anyone had asked, and it sort of shook me. So the nurse got bossy. She sent me for scans and the radiographer told me to take a few deep breaths and relax. And I lay there and listened to my baby's heartbeat, and suddenly it was real. I was having a baby.'

'Our baby,' he said softly.

There was a long silence. *Our baby.* How loaded were those two words?

'I think that was in the mix too,' she whispered at last. 'Yours and mine. What we had…it was good, Marc.'

'It was.'

'But I was still planning on adoption,' she told him. 'I remember lying there thinking, *He's real. He was conceived out of love. He has to go to a wonderful home.* And then the radiographer's wand reached his feet.'

'Which were clubbed.'

'I could see them,' she whispered. 'I could see how badly they were clubbed. And of course I'd done two years of medicine. I knew what he'd be facing, but I also knew there was the chance of more.'

Marc did too. Of course he did. Club feet were sometimes associated with other problems. He thought them through and they weren't pretty. Trisomy 18 syndrome. Distal arthrogryposis. Myotonic dystrophy. The chance of each of those was small, but real.

'I know it's only twenty per cent of cases,' she told him. 'Club feet are usually the only presenting condition, but that was enough. I lay there and watched his image and thought, *Who do I trust to look after my baby?* Because suddenly he was *my* baby. And there was no need to answer, because by the time I walked out of that room no one was going to have the chance.'

He understood. He hated probing more, but he had to have answers. 'So you decided to keep him—but you also decided not to tell me?'

'How could I? I'd been following the situation in Falkenstein. I'd seen the war shattering your country. I'd even seen you on the news, working in a field hospital, talking to reporters of the struggles you were having after so many months, with the international community losing interest, with winter coming, with so many homeless. I knew you felt guilty about me anyway, so why hang more guilt on you? You'd agreed to adoption so why not just let you think he was adopted? What's the difference, Marc, between someone unknown taking care of our son and me?'

'For a start I would have funded you.'

'I didn't need funding. You sent me two years' income and paid the rest of my university fees. You insisted I keep that. What more could I ask?'

'That I care for my son!' The shock, the frustration, the rage that he'd kept at bay all day suddenly vented itself in those six fierce words. He slammed his fist on the table so hard that the salt and pepper shakers toppled and rolled to the floor.

Neither of them noticed.

His rage was so great he could scarcely contain it, but it wasn't rage at Ellie. It was rage at himself.

He hadn't enquired. He hadn't followed up.

What sort of low-life left a woman with a baby and didn't find out how she was—for nine years?

'Marc, you did ask,' Ellie whispered, and her response shocked him. It was as if she guessed what he was thinking. 'You rang after Felix was born.'

He remembered the call.

He'd spent the night operating in a field hospital after yet another bomb blast had shattered lives. He'd come back to his quarters to find the email, telling him that he had a son. He'd driven for hours to the nearest place there was reception, trying to put a call through. When he'd finally reached her, Ellie had sounded tired, spent, but okay.

'He's a beautiful little boy, Marc. You can be proud. He'll have a good home, I promise. Yes, I'm okay and amazingly Mum's okay too. She's had another transplant and this one looks like it's taken. My plan is to go back to university and Mum's promised to help. No, there's nothing

you can do. Would you like me to send you a photograph of your—? Of the baby?'

And, idiot that he was, he'd said no. He'd wanted no picture of his son. How many times had he regretted it? But after having said it—that he didn't want the hurt of seeing what could have been—how could he turn back?

The events of the last few days—the royal tragedy, his ascension to the throne, things that had seemed overwhelming—were suddenly nothing.

He'd walked out on his wife, she'd borne him a son and she'd kept him. She was here now, and his son was right through the door, dreaming of splash-lubricated crankshafts and magneto ignition...*and a father who might share his life.*

Ellie was looking at him as if she was scared. What, that he'd hit her? Sure, he was angry. He had every right to be, but he wasn't angry at Ellie.

He'd been a doctor for years. How many times had he seen the grief of a lost baby? How could he not have guessed that a decision taken when Ellie had first learned she was pregnant couldn't be carried through when she'd held her son in her arms?

Once she'd known her baby had formation issues she could never have given him away. She'd have fought for him to the death.

But that was the Ellie he'd known then. The Ellie he looked at now seemed as if the fight had been knocked out of her.

'Marc, why are you here?' she whispered and he struggled to swallow self-loathing and answer.

'Why did you call him Felix?' he asked tangentially.

'It means lucky. Blessed. When I first saw him, I swore that's what he'd be.'

'If he has you for a mum, that's a given.'

But she shook her head. 'Marc, don't. I don't need compliments. What was between us was over nine years ago. I haven't heard from you since our divorce. I assumed you'd have a wife and kids by now and be ruling the health system of Falkenstein. I've searched for you on the Internet from time to time,' she confessed. 'You seem to have been doing really well. I'm sorry about your dad, by the way. Heart attack?'

She'd been keeping tabs on him while he'd blocked her out completely. That made him feel even worse.

What did he know about her?

Involuntarily, he checked her ring finger. There was nothing there.

He thought of the ring that had once lain there—his great-grandmother's, a ring of beauty and antiquity. Ellie had returned it after the divorce but he'd sent it straight back.

'I want you to keep it, Ellie. You're a woman of honour and I'm sure my great-grandmother would be proud if you kept wearing it. Move it to another finger and wear it with pride.'

Why would she still be wearing it?

No reason at all.

What had she asked? His father. A heart attack. 'Yes. It was sudden. He was still working full-time.' He hesitated. 'Your mum?'

'She died five years ago. The first transplant lasted three years, the second one four. It was a good four years, though. She loved Felix and helped me care for him.'

'And you managed to get through university.'

'Somehow. We eked out your money. I had a room in Sydney where we all stayed. Mum looked after Felix as best she could. When she couldn't, I'd bring them both back here. I made a deal with the town—if they helped me with Felix and Mum, I'd come back and be the local doctor.'

'But you wanted to specialise.'

'Family practice is a specialty.'

'But it's not what you wanted.'

'So I've learned we can't always have what we want.' She looked directly at him. 'What do you want, Marc?'

And how much would he have given to be able to say he didn't want anything? That this was a spur-of-the-moment visit, popping in to visit his ex-wife who he hoped could still be a friend.

Ha.

'I needed to see you,' he tried.

She looked at him directly and shrugged. 'No. We're over that long since. Didn't we figure need was another name for lust?'

'What was between us wasn't just lust.'

'No. It was a juvenile love affair. But I'm asking again, Marc. Why are you here? I thought it must be that you learned about me keeping Felix, but by your reaction it seems it's not. So, you happened to be visiting Australia and decided to see how much your ex-wife has aged? What?'

There was no easy way to say this. *Just say it, Marc.*

'I came because the entire Falkenstein royal family died in a plane crash. Three days ago I was fourth in line for the throne. Now the crown is mine.'

Her face creased in shock. 'That's appalling. Why wasn't it on the news? Or maybe it was. I've been so busy.' And then her face softened. 'They're your family. Marc, I'm so sorry.'

'I don't need sympathy,' he said roughly. 'There's never been any love lost between us. I've always kept as far from the palace as possible. But now...'

'Now?' She took a moment to take in the full implications of what he'd said. 'You're...you're the new King?'

'Yes.'

Her face changed again, becoming wary. 'And that means...what? Why are you here?'

There was no way to soften what needed to be said.

'I travelled all this way, fast, to ask you to keep Felix's adoption records quiet,' he told her. 'There's already intense media interest in an obscure doctor who's suddenly their monarch. Enough people know of our short marriage that it can't be hidden. I hoped, however, that the birth would go unnoticed, or at least you could hide the adoption details.'

'Why?'

'Because adoption is accepted as legal abdication,' he said heavily. 'According to our constitution, if Felix had been formally adopted at birth he'd have no rights to succession but the media interest could still be upsetting. Now...'

Marc paused, overwhelmed by what he had to tell her.

Ellie rose and opened the sideboard. She poured two whiskies. Large ones.

'I don't drink this except in emergencies,' she told him. 'I suspect I need it now. Maybe we both do. So tell me.'

He took the glass and drained it, and then he looked at Ellie.

He could still see the girl he'd loved behind those tired eyes. He could still see the laughter, the fun... But he could also see the care and the responsibility.

When their world had crashed, she'd looked at things dispassionately.

'You're needed where you are and so am I. Our marriage was a fantasy and we need to put it behind us. Good luck, Marc, and goodbye.'

He watched her shoulders brace yet again, and he hated it.

'Ellie, I'm now the Crown Prince of Falkenstein and Felix is my son. It takes a year to formalise a divorce in Australia so Felix was born while we were still legally married. This may mess with all our lives in ways I can't imagine but, once I'm crowned, Felix will take my current title. Your son—*our* son—will be the new Crown Prince of Falkenstein.'

CHAPTER FOUR

SILENCE. IT STRETCHED on and on, deep and threatening. The shock seemed endless.

Marc thought of his stupefaction when he'd first learned of this, and he thought it must be the same or even greater for Ellie.

One of the reasons he'd loved her was her courage. How much courage did she need to face this?

'I don't think I like this,' she whispered at last. And then she looked up and met his gaze head-on. 'That's an understatement. It terrifies me.'

'I remember when you first found out I was a prince.'

'That terrified me too.'

'Enough to end our marriage.'

'Is that fair?' she snapped. 'We were in a bubble and suddenly everything burst. The war in your country, finding out you were a prince, Mum's illness… Why didn't you even tell me you were a prince?'

'Because I didn't feel like one. I never did.' He'd tried to explain it then, but she'd been too angry, too confused. And he understood. Their short marriage had seemed idyllic, but suddenly there were images of war. The international spotlight shining on a country that had almost escaped the notice of the world in general had been bad enough, but superimposed on that was the news that Ellie's mother was fighting for her life.

In the face of her mother's illness she'd turned to him for support, and he'd had to point to the headlines and tell her he had to go home.

And tell her why. That he was indeed a prince. That his father was trying to hold the country's health service together. That the need was desperate.

He looked at her now and saw the same look of betrayal that he'd seen then. She'd understood why he'd needed to return to his country. What she hadn't forgiven was that he hadn't told her he was royal.

'The title of Prince remains for two generations,' he told her now. 'So yes, I'm a prince. My father used his title only because it gave him authority as head of the country's health system, but as a kid it only gave me grief. I dropped it.'

'But you can't lose it altogether.'

'I can't,' he told her. 'Not officially. And now neither can Felix. Because he's third generation, he's not had a title up until now, but Ellie, I'm sorry, that's changed. He's the new Crown Prince.'

'He's a little boy,' she said, sounding desperate. 'He's a country kid who's just coming out of a childhood marred by operation after operation for feet that don't work.' She closed her eyes and he saw a wash of anguish. 'You can't take him, Marc. I won't let you.'

'Is that why you think I'm here? To take my son? I won't take him from you.'

But, even as he said it, the words slammed home a truth impossible to ignore. *My son.* He had a son.

A kid with courage and humour and intelligence. A son to be proud of.

Like Ellie… She'd been a wife to be proud of.

'So where does that leave us?' she demanded. 'Am I to hide him? Is that what you want? What, Marc? What demands does your country make of you—of us—now?'

'That's not fair.'

'It is fair,' she flashed. 'An accident of birth made you Prince of a country I'd never heard of and then a stupid war that achieved nothing killed our marriage. And now the death of a man you say you had nothing to do with has catapulted you into a role I don't understand. Do you even want it?'

And there was the Ellie he knew. He remembered that about her, that she always saw behind the façade. He'd come to Australia fresh out of medical school, determined to have fun, sow a few wild oats before he settled down to the grim struggle he knew was facing him. But as soon as he'd met Ellie he'd forgotten the wild oats. She seemed to see inside his soul.

He'd had more fun with her than he'd ever dreamed of, but it had been gentle fun, dictated by her need to study. It had been working through her texts with her. It had been swimming at Bondi, ducking each other in the waves, slapping on not enough sunscreen. It had been massaging each other with after-sun lotion, slowly, languorously.

It had been waking in each other's arms.

Now, looking across the table at her, he remembered every moment, and the rush of sudden desire almost blindsided him. *Ellie. His wife.*

'Don't,' she said and he knew she'd seen it too. 'Don't even think about going there. Get back to what matters. You've inherited the throne. You don't want it? Why can't you abdicate?'

'Because my grandfather propelled us into a war that almost destroyed my country.' Somehow he hauled himself back to the issue at hand. He'd had enough time on the long flight out here to accept the inevitable. 'Because another cousin will inherit if I don't accept, and Ranald's a battle-hungry fool. There's always been conflict on our eastern border and Ranald would see himself as a general, ordering our people to fight.'

'But now Felix stands between Ranald and the throne?'

'I can abdicate for myself but not for Felix. If I abdicate, Ranald will be Prince Regent. He would have a say in how Felix is raised. He'd be in control.'

'I get to say how Felix is raised.'

There were more things that had to be said. 'Ellie, succession's vital for the stability of the country and the region. In the circumstances, Ranald could apply to an international court for Felix's custody. He might even win.'

There was an angry gasp. She was thinking fast. He could see it.

And she saw the next chasm.

'If Ranald could apply for custody and win, that means you could demand it too.'

'I suspect so.' He couldn't deny it.

'But you don't want him. You never wanted him!'

This was beyond impossible. Did he want his son? He thought again of Ellie's long-ago message telling him of Felix's birth. The pain had been unbearable—was still unbearable. Ellie and his baby were all he'd ever wanted and he'd had to turn his back.

But there was no turning his back on this situation. Did the stability of the country demand he tear his son from his mother? He needed to talk to the lawyers back at home, figure out the implications.

He needed to find a nice, peaceful operating theatre and do something tricky, like repairing that elbow this afternoon. Strangely, that had settled him. It had taken all his concentration but by the time he'd walked out of Theatre the shock of seeing Ellie—and Felix—had somehow been put into perspective.

So now what? He could hardly demand that a gall bladder repair appear on cue. Ellie was looking at him for answers, and she needed them now.

Ellie. The woman who'd been his wife.

What had he done to her?

'I won't take Felix,' he told her and, despite the complications, despite the massive uproar he foresaw when Felix's existence was discovered, he knew that this was his line in the sand. 'Felix is your son and his upbringing is your business. But...'

'But?'

He took a deep breath. 'This will take some getting your head around,' he told her. 'But Felix stands to inherit the throne and until he's of an age where he can decide for himself, there's nothing we can do about it.'

'Which means...'

'Which means we tell him. Which means we introduce him to his country.'

'He's not leaving here.'

'Not permanently. But at first... Ellie, how do you feel about bringing him to Falkenstein for the coronation? Let the people see him. Let the media talk openly about what happened between us. Introduce Felix to his people with all honour.'

'His people...' She seemed dazed.

'The more I think about it, the more it seems the only way. Otherwise you'll have the media filling in gaps with speculation. The coronation's at the end of next month. You'd need to come a few weeks beforehand so Felix can get his head around what's expected of him. Then we can ask for media cooperation to leave Felix be until he reaches maturity. We could arrange for a photo shoot once a year—maybe you could bring him over to the palace for your summer holidays. But he'll mostly be here, out of the spotlight.'

'But not now.' It was practically a wail. 'He can't travel. His leg... The risk of thrombosis...'

'We can pay for the whole of first class if we need—or hire our own jet. That'll give him more than enough room to move around and negate the risk of a clot.'

'You're kidding.'

'Felix is a prince,' he said gently. 'You need to get used to it.'

'But I'd have to come with him.'

'You would,' he agreed gravely. 'It'd be overwhelming for a nine-year-old to face without his mother.'

'I can't.'

'Because?' He was watching her face, watching anguish. 'Ellie, you couldn't come with me before because of your mother, and because you needed to finish your medical training. I'm not asking you to return as my wife. I'm asking you to come for a few weeks. What's stopping you?'

'I couldn't come then for all sorts of reasons,' she snapped, anguish veering towards anger. 'You were flying back into a war zone. I was a student. I had no skills to help. What was I supposed to do, sit back and play doctor's wife while you played the hero?'

'Ellie...'

'It was all sorts of impossible,' she flashed. 'And it's impossible now. I'm a country doctor. This is where I'm needed. I can't just leave for what...six weeks?'

'There must be some way...'

'Even if there was I wouldn't take it. You broke my heart once. You think I'd let you do it again?'

And that was a conversation-changer.

'This isn't about us,' he managed.

'No,' she flashed. 'And it's not going to be. There's nothing between us and there's nothing between you and your son. As far as you were concerned, for the last nine years we haven't existed.'

'That's not true.'

'It has to be true. I'm the only doctor in this place. I'm needed here, and Felix needs to be here too. His leg—'

'There are specialists in Falkenstein.'

'I'm not listening. I'm not going. Bring on your lawyers, Marc, because I'll fight you every inch of the way.'

'Ellie, see reason.'

'I am seeing reason.' Her green eyes were flashing fire and suddenly the years fell away. This was the Ellie he knew.

He remembered the first time he'd met her. She'd been in a waitress uniform, a silly, frilly apron and a cap that was slightly skewed with her auburn hair escaping from the regulation knot. She'd been surrounded by a sea of wine and broken glass. He'd caught her shoulders to stop her falling.

He'd been wearing a dinner jacket and a crisp white shirt. His shirt had suddenly looked like a kindergarten finger painting. She'd gazed at him in horror, but then, just for a moment, their gazes had locked.

'Whoops,' she'd said and it had been all he could do not to laugh. Amazingly, her eyes had twinkled back.

Then she'd swung into penitent mode, and gratitude that he'd accepted the blame, but her first reaction had been laughter. It had been that twinkle, that defiance in seeing the funny side in what should, for her, have been a catastrophe, that made him wait for her that night.

The defiance was here now. But not the humour.

'Go away, Marc. This is scaring me to death.'

'The Ellie I knew had courage.'

'I'm not the Ellie you knew.'

'Ellie, the royal thing…' How to make her see? 'It's just like Felix's club feet. It's non-negotiable. It's something we have to deal with.'

'You deal with it. Leave us alone.'

He raked his hair.

But there were other things now that were messing with his head. He'd almost forgotten how much this woman had meant to him. He'd almost forgotten how much he wanted her.

They were feelings he couldn't possibly admit to now. He gazed across to her in baffled silence. Where to go from here?

Maybe it would have been best to send a lawyer, he

thought. A lawyer could spell things out without emotion. Emotions were doing his head in. He needed help.

But so did Ellie, far more than him. He looked at her tired face and he tried to look dispassionately. Tried to see the big picture.

'Ellie, why are you working here on your own?' he said tangentially. 'Why are you looking as if you haven't had enough sleep for weeks?'

'Maybe I haven't.'

'So the practice is too big for one doctor?'

'I— Yes, it is.'

'Then why…?'

'Because Felix costs me a fortune.' She might not have said it if she hadn't been pushed close to the edge, he thought. He remembered her flat refusal to accept financial aid once their marriage had ended and he realised this admission, for Ellie, was huge. 'His specialist…the operations… This isn't a rich district and people often can't afford to pay but I promised…'

And anger surged again.

'Then that stops now,' he said flatly. 'I owe you for ten years of child maintenance for a start. I can afford to pay for locums, starting now. You will accept help, Ellie.'

'You can't buy me.'

'I'm not buying. I'm paying what I owe. Ellie…'

But she'd had enough. She ran her fingers through her hair in a gesture of pure exhaustion and it was all he could do not to reach out and take her hand in his. To reassure her.

But he'd frightened her to death and reassurance wasn't possible.

'Go away, Marc,' she managed.

'You know I can't do that.'

'Then go…I don't know…wherever you're staying. I need space. I need to think.'

'We can sort this out.'

'Maybe, but I need to get my head clear,' she snapped.

'You've had time to come to terms with this. I haven't.' She took a deep breath. 'Tomorrow, I have clinic…'

'Could I help?'

'You've helped enough.' She rose and opened the door into the night. 'I finish clinic at midday. I usually eat lunch here but if you buy me sandwiches we can talk during lunch.'

'I could—'

'That's all, Marc,' she said flatly, drearily. 'Please. Let me be.'

And he looked at her for a long moment, but there was nothing for him to do except leave.

There were sheep in the paddock beside the motel, snuffling and bleating under his window.

It wasn't the sheep keeping him awake.

He felt as if he'd been picked up and placed into a parallel universe.

A universe where he had a son.

He'd always known Felix existed but there'd been a job opening as a father nine years ago, and he'd missed it.

'I couldn't have come,' he said out loud into the dark. 'Even if I'd known Ellie was doing the parenting…'

Ellie.

Why was the image of Ellie's face, Ellie's shock, Ellie's weariness, superimposed on every other thought?

His phone buzzed. Josef.

The explanation of what had happened left the old man stunned.

'You have a legitimate heir? Do you realise what uproar this will cause? You need to bring him home. Is your ex-wife reasonable? Does she agree?'

'I don't know,' he said heavily. 'To be honest, I don't know anything about her. Give me time.'

'You have two days. Has she remarried?'

'No.'

'So why did you divorce? Would it be possible to re-marry?' Josef sounded so stunned he was clutching at straws. 'No matter. You do need to marry but that can be sorted later and you obviously can't remarry if she's unsuitable. What's important now is to get the child here any way you can but, whatever you do, keep your ex-wife onside. The last thing you need is a tell-all exposé in the press.'

'I'll do my best.'

'Promise her anything within reason. The last thing we need is more scandal. Give her anything she wants.'

He disconnected and lay there, staring into the dark.

Give her anything she wants?

I'll do my best.

Ellie had received a lot less than his best in the past. What made him think she'd accept any more now?

And in her hospital apartment Ellie lay and looked sightlessly into the same dark.

Marc was here.

She'd thought she was over him. How could the sight of him sitting at her kitchen table do her head in?

Marc belonged to a crazy time in her life. For a short few months she'd forgotten the responsibilities life had thrust on her almost as soon as she was able to walk. An invalid mother who'd refused to take care of herself. A father who'd walked out on them. A town who'd helped her train and expected medical care in return.

She buried her head in the pillows but it didn't help. She climbed out of bed and went and stared out of the window into the dark.

Marc was just down the road, in the local motel. Marc, the most gorgeous man she'd ever set eyes on. The man who'd turned her world upside down.

Who'd just turned it upside down again.

Be practical. She forced herself to put aside the image

of her ex-husband—tricky that—and focus on what he was asking of her.

Could she go to Falkenstein?

'It might be exciting,' she muttered. 'Maybe I'd get to stay in a palace.'

'Felix would stay in the palace.' She was arguing with herself. 'They'd probably put me in an attic. But an attic in Falkenstein might be more exciting than here.'

'Oh, for heaven's sake...' She threw the window open so the night air could cool her heated face. The night was full of the vision of Marc. Her head felt as if it might explode.

To take Felix to Falkenstein, or to let him go without her. To lose control.

The alternative, to spend weeks near Marc...

The in-house phone rang, the connection between her apartment and the hospital, and she almost fell on it with relief. Anything to stop herself thinking of Marc.

The nurse was apologetic. 'Ellie? Sorry to wake you but Mrs Ferguson's restless. Permission to up the diazepam?'

An intercom in Felix's room connected to the nurses' station meant she could come and go to the hospital without worrying. 'Yes! I'll come.'

'There's no need,' the nurse said, startled. 'If you can just give me a phone order... She's not uncomfortable, just doing her usual moaning, but she's getting loud.'

That wasn't so unusual. Eighty years old and in hospital because she'd broken her foot while trying to kick her son's dog, Myra Ferguson moaned at the world.

But Ellie had the choice. She could stay here staring into the dark or she could go and hear how appalling the world was treating Myra and how inconsiderate her son was to own a dog.

There wasn't a choice. The dark involved thinking of Marc.

Myra's moans were nothing in comparison.

CHAPTER FIVE

SOMETIMES ELLIE'S CLINICS ran over time. Often. Sometimes she finished her morning clinic to find her afternoon patients already queueing.

But not this morning. She ushered out her last patient and her receptionist was beaming.

'All done, and not a single house call. And your gorgeous doctor friend is waiting in the car park. You should see the car he's driving! It's a bright red sports car, and he has the sun roof down. He's about to whisk you off to an assignation.'

'Sandwiches and soda in the park,' she said dryly. 'I'll be back in thirty minutes.'

'I've cleared an hour if you need it,' Marilyn said serenely. 'Oh, Ellie, he's beautiful. And the rumours are that he's Felix's father.'

This town! Word would have flown throughout the district before breakfast.

'You want to put a bit of lippy on?' Marilyn said happily. 'And unfasten that top button.'

'Oh, for heaven's sake…'

But she did just happen to glance in the mirror before she left. A woman had some pride.

What had happened to her in the past ten years?

He watched her walk towards him and he worried.

She was wearing faded black pants, a white shirt and a soft grey cardigan. Plain black shoes, old. Her auburn hair was caught into a sensible knot.

She wore no make-up, no jewellery.

She looked as if she'd turned into a workhorse. His beautiful, vibrant Ellie…

He'd done this to her. He'd turned her into a single parent.

Maybe he should be angry that she'd kept things from him, and part of him was, but the overwhelming feeling he had was guilt.

And grief.

'Do you have sandwiches or will I grab some from the hospital kitchen?' she called, and he thought, great, he'd eaten her fish and chips and now she was offering to bring hospital sandwiches. What would he give to be able to say he had a picnic basket loaded with lobster, caviar, the finest selection of breads from a French *boulangerie*, champagne on ice…?

'I have pies,' he told her. 'Courtesy of the general store. And fruit and soda.' How exotic was that? What was the use in being King? he thought ruefully. He should have called for the army to fly in truffles before dawn.

But it seemed they were acceptable. 'Pies?' Her face lit and he thought, *Wow*. What a small thing to give her pleasure.

And why did that make him feel so good?

'Mrs Thomas makes the best pies,' she told him as she reached him. 'You can't think how tired I get of hospital food, but there's seldom enough time for me to cook or even shop. There's a park down by the creek and the creek has water at this time of year. I have my phone. We might get lucky and it'll stay silent long enough for us to eat.'

'I need time to talk.'

'I know,' she told him and slid into his car. 'So talk.'

But he couldn't for a bit. The pleasure on her face had unsettled him. Disarmed him even.

He followed her directions down to what she'd optimistically referred to as a park—a stand of gum trees on a bend in a creek bed. They set themselves up on the lone park bench. He handed Ellie a pie and she attacked it as if there was no tomorrow.

'You were hungry?' he asked, startled, and she smiled between mouthfuls.

'I'm experienced,' she told him. 'My beeper goes and my food gets forgotten. I learned early to feed rather than graze.'

'Just how busy are you?'

'Twenty-four-seven.' She paused and looked down at the remains of her pie with respect. 'But I do get fed. The hospital cook has been known to show up when I'm inundated with house calls. I'll come out of someone's front door and she'll be standing there with a plate of lasagne and arms akimbo, glaring at me and daring me not to eat before I go to the next job. They look after me,' she said simply. 'It's why I'm here. This town is desperate for a doctor and they'll do what they must to keep me. Including looking after Felix. I've never had to worry about childcare. As a single mum, I have it easy.'

'You don't look like you have it easy.'

'We're not here to talk about me. We need to talk about Felix.'

'Ellie...'

'We'll come,' she said simply. 'I'll accept your help finding locums. I understand this is Felix's life. I can't refuse. But I won't leave him there, Marc. He comes home with me after the coronation. He can spend a couple of weeks every year with you, as long as I have your written assurance, overseen by international lawyers, that he returns to Australia after each two weeks away. When he's eighteen, he can make up his own mind what to do.'

So he'd got what he wanted. Sort of.

'You'll come with him?'

'For the first visit, yes, but for the rest, as long as you make sure he's safely escorted and cared for, my place is here.'

'He'll need to come a bit before. There'll be a media frenzy. We need to prepare you both.'

'We?'

'The royal minders. They'll also be preparing me for my role but that's not...'

'My business? No.' Her mouth set. 'He'll need to stay at the palace?'

'Yes.'

'I can stay with him?'

'I hope you will.'

'I can't imagine me in a palace.'

'I can't imagine me in a palace,' he told her and she looked swiftly up at him.

'You don't want this?'

'What do you think?'

She stared up at him for a long moment. 'I guess...I don't know anything at all about you, Marc. Or make that Your Highness. I know nothing at all.'

'You knew enough to marry me.'

'I was nineteen years old. A lovestruck teenager.'

'And you've regretted it ever since?'

Why had he asked? What difference did it make? Was it vanity—or something else?

When the thought of marriage had come up it had seemed impossible, fraught with problems, a fairy tale. But the day after Ellie's exams, he'd woken with her beside him. He'd lain in the filtered dawn light and thought of the last weeks, during which he should have been travelling, enjoying the freedom he'd craved. Instead of which, he'd stayed in Ellie's bedsit, helping her cram, or walking her to and from her endless waitressing jobs, or thinking of what to make for dinner   and actually cooking! He'd swotted up on student medicine—the things he'd had to learn for exams but had promptly forgotten the moment he'd passed. He'd pushed her, bullied her, hugged her, worried with her...

And that morning she'd woken in his arms and he'd kissed her and said, 'Ellie, I know marriage is impossible but dammit, let's do it anyway. Let's face the impossible afterwards.' She'd kissed him and said a drowsy, deliriously happy yes. And four weeks later, despite the sonorous drone of the marriage celebrant intoning the age-old vows in a council chamber, those vows had seemed like life itself.

For as long as you both shall live...

Maybe that was why he'd never thought of marrying again.

And you've regretted it ever since? His question hung in the air between them.

'I have Felix,' she said and bit into her remaining pie with a decisive crunch. 'How can I regret that?'

That was enough to shut him up. It wasn't about him. It was about a son he'd never known.

'What about you?' she said as she demolished the last crust and looked consideringly at the apple he'd provided. 'I'm not asking if you regret our marriage. That's a given— apart from Felix it was an appalling mistake. But wife? Kids? Why not?'

'No time.'

'Like me.'

'And you've been working too hard so you can pay for Felix's medical costs. And your mother's too, I'll bet. Ellie, why the hell didn't you tell me?' It was an explosion and a couple of ducks that had been edging nearer, eyeing crusts, took to the air in flight.

'It wasn't your business.'

'Of course it was my business.'

She'd picked up the apple. Now she laid it back down on

the bench and stood and faced him. 'I lied to you,' she told him. 'Oh, I didn't tell outright lies but I let you believe Felix had been adopted. That was deceit. And at first I did it to protect you. I was reading about the situation in Falkenstein and I knew the pressure you were under. I knew how impossible it would be for you to drop everything and come. But afterwards, when the war ended...'

'Yes?' He was still angry, still frustrated. She was standing before him, a shadow of the vibrant girl he'd married. She was weary, careworn, worried. Her hair could do with a cut. Her clothes were...serviceable.

Half his frustration was that he wanted to pick her up and change things. Give her time to sleep. Send her to a decent hairdresser. Buy her some attractive clothes.

Care for her...

'I was afraid you'd still care,' she said and it brought him up short. 'I was afraid...the feelings we had...they were so strong they threw our lives out of control. My mum needed me. The town needed me and Felix needed me. When I was with you I forgot everything and it scared me witless. I couldn't go there again. I couldn't risk it. I thought, if I told you, you'd come. You were honourable, you'd want a say in how Felix was raised, but most of all you'd be in my life. I couldn't afford to feel like that.' She took a deep breath. 'And, Marc, I still can't.'

And he understood.

Anger faded as he faced her fear head-on. He thought of the times he'd wanted to contact her, to find out how her life was going. He thought of the times he'd come close and then pulled away.

He had no life to offer a bride. Even now. The goldfish bowl of royalty, the appalling media attention he was about to attract, the resentment the people had for a royal family who'd brought them nothing but trouble—combined, it was the stuff of nightmares.

He thought fleetingly of Josef's assertion...

'We need to find you a wife. Get you a son...'

What a joke! There was so much to do to put the country back on a stable footing, how could he possibly have time to woo and wed a suitable bride?

Fraught as things were, Felix at least answered this problem. He now had a son.

He didn't need a wife. He could stay in control. Sort of.

Ellie was looking straight at him, her gaze defiant. What she'd said had been a confession of sorts, he thought. A confirmation that what had been between them was a wildfire, impossible to control.

But, like a wildfire, even though the flames were long gone, embers glowed underground for years, awaiting their chance to flare again.

'I get it,' he said roughly. 'I don't have to like it, but I understand. But you'll let me help now. You'll come back here after the coronation, but from now on the financial responsibility for Felix is mine. He's to receive the best medical care available and you—Ellie, you're officially mother to the Crown Prince and as such you'll receive an allowance.'

'I don't want your money.'

'It's not my money. It's a state allowance for the Crown Prince and his mother, and it's not negotiable. I *will* care for you.' There was that anger again. The wildfire analogy flashed back—an ember smouldering deep underground.

He caught himself. He gathered the remains of the picnic and carried it to the trash can. When he returned, Ellie was still standing, watching him. Her face was expressionless but he knew this woman.

Was he seeing fear?

'Ellie…' He reached out and touched her face, but she slapped his hand away as if he were a viper.

'Don't touch me.'

'I didn't mean—'

'Neither of us meant anything. What happened between us was stupid on so many levels.'

'We loved each other.'

'Did either of us know what love is? I loved my mum and she needed me. You loved your country and you were needed at home. Now I love Felix. That's the love we need to focus on. What was between us was crazy, a stupid denial of responsibilities.'

He watched her face and still saw fear, but also the wash of raw emotion she couldn't conceal. His presence was re-awakening something she had no control over and he understood. He felt the same.

Ten years ago he'd fallen for this woman in a way he could never understand, and somewhere under the fear, despite the years of separation, that incomprehensible feeling still lingered.

But it had to be ignored. For one crazy moment he thought about what it would be like to be a medieval royal prince. He could summon his knights, point to Ellie and say *I'll have that one.* His knights would carry her to his bed. His women would bathe her and dress her as she deserved to be dressed. All honour would be bestowed on her and she'd be his Queen.

Yeah. Like that was going to happen. The time for impulse, for passion was over. For behind Ellie's fear there was anger. Ellie's life was here. He was messing with it enough. He couldn't risk pushing it further.

'I won't touch you,' he told her.

But was that enough? She was staring at him as if baffled.

'What?'

'I have no idea,' she snapped. 'I don't have a clue what I'm feeling, much less why. All I know is that you lay a hand on me and all deals are off. I'll fight you every inch of the way for Felix, and maybe you'll win because you have the resources to fight, but I'll try anyway. And you won't make friends with Felix that way. If you want to be his dad, you respect my boundaries.'

'Of course.'

But even then she was looking at him as if he was some kind of puzzle she couldn't work out.

Her phone buzzed. She glanced at it and he saw relief.

'I need to go. Rebecca Taylor's parents have just brought her in and Chris thinks it's appendicitis. If Chris thinks it's appendix, it's ninety nine per cent sure to be appendix.'

And wasn't that just what he needed? Medicine. Something he understood. 'Would you like me to help?'

'No!'

'You can't operate on your own.'

'Chris will help if necessary but I'll try and settle things, and evacuate her to the city.'

'I'm a surgeon. You know as well as I do that sometimes an appendix can turn into an emergency. Let me check.'

Her expression changed, from defensive to understanding and sympathy.

'You want to work.'

There was no response but the truth. 'Yes.'

'Marc...' He saw compassion in her eyes. 'They're asking you to give up medicine?'

'I have no choice.'

'Again?'

'What's that supposed to mean?'

She shook her head. 'You had no choice when you walked away from us. If that hurt you as much as it hurt me...' She paused, catching herself. 'No matter. That's history. But for you to walk away from your medicine as well as everything else...'

'I can handle it.'

'I'm sure you can,' she whispered. 'But oh, Marc, it'll hurt.' She considered for a moment and then came to a decision. 'Okay. Yesterday we worked on emergency principles. In a life or death situation a doctor can't be sued. An overseas doctor can step in at need. Today's probably not an emergency, but if you work as my official assistant—under supervision—there shouldn't be a problem.'

Ellie's assistant… It sounded good to him.

'There's nothing I'd like better.'

'Then don't smile at me like that,' she snapped, suddenly angry. 'Because when you do—'

'When I do—what?'

'When you do, I feel like I have no business to feel what I feel,' she managed and her voice wobbled. 'Marc, I have no intention of ever feeling like I did ten years ago, but we *can* work together. Let's see to this appendix and then move on.'

Rebecca Taylor was thirteen years old and terrified. She was retching when Marc and Ellie walked into the ward. When the retching eased she cringed back into herself, folding into the foetal position.

'Hey,' Ellie said, stooping and brushing her hair from the girl's face, removing the bowl, putting her face at the level of Rebecca's. She had obviously been retching for a while; she was producing nothing. 'Becky, hugs. This is horrid. We're here to get it sorted, to get this pain to stop. Do you mind if Dr Falken takes a look at you? He's a surgeon. He's also my friend, and he's good.'

The words gave Marc a jolt. *He's also my friend, and he's good.* It was a normal thing for one doctor to say of a colleague. Why did it sound different coming from Ellie? Why did it sound…more?

He glanced at Becky's parents and saw their shoulders ease. The way Ellie had introduced him was a reassurance all on its own.

And, through her pain, Becky's attention was caught. 'He's the doc from yesterday? The one they're all talking about?' Despite her distress she looked across at Marc. 'He's…he's cute.'

'He is, isn't he?' Ellie said smoothly. 'And he's a very

good doctor. He's a surgeon, which I'm not, and we think you may have appendicitis, which is something surgeons are good at. I'll stay with you, but is it okay if Dr Falken examines you?'

The fear surged back. 'Mum?'

Becky's mum took her daughter's hand. 'You can do this, Becky,' she whispered. 'Relax and let Dr Falken fix the problem.'

'Let's see your tummy,' Marc told her. 'Becky, I need you to tell me if my hands are cold. I'm known for warm hands but sometimes my central heating lets me down. Chris has told you she thinks it's appendicitis? You know you don't need your appendix. You would if you were a rabbit and ate grass but I can't see you as a grass-eating type of girl. If you let me check your tummy, and I find that Chris is right, it's simply a matter of popping you to sleep, nicking the appendix out and popping it into a jar so you can gross out your friends. Then you get a couple of weeks off school while your mum and dad spoil you rotten. Would that be okay?'

He had Becky mesmerised. She gave him a weak smile and managed to roll so her tummy was available for inspection. 'You heard that, Mum?' she whispered. 'Would that mean a new video game? Of my choice?'

'I guess,' her mum said with a wavering smile at her husband. 'If that's what the doctor says.'

'That's what both doctors say,' Ellie told them. 'Thanks, Becky. Okay, Dr Falken, rub those hands until they're warm and let's get on with it.'

Marc gently probed Becky's abdomen. She let him press and then cried out in pain as he released the pressure.

Rebound.

Ellie had thought she was doing Marc a favour by asking him to help, but now the favour was reversed. Rebound was a sign that the appendix had burst. She could send Becky to Sydney but the longer they waited the more the infected matter would spread.

So once again Marc was in the operating theatre. This time Ellie gave the anaesthetic while Chris assisted.

Becky was a healthy thirteen-year-old. Anaesthetising and intubating was relatively straightforward. Ellie had time to watch.

There was no doubting this man was good. His fingers were nimble, sure, skilled as he removed the mess of an appendix. There was no hesitation. If she'd had to operate she'd have struggled. Someone more skilled might well have had to go in after her.

Oh, to have someone like this working beside her.

And that made her think. *To work beside Marc every day...*

That had been a dream from a long time ago. Some time during their honeymoon—a few days spent on the beach at Bondi—they'd planned a future where they set up a hospital together, where they worked side by side, where they were partners in every sense of the word.

But then the world had stepped in, as it had stepped in again now.

What Marc was doing was brilliant. He'd removed the gangrenous appendix and was cleaning the cavity with scrupulous care. He couldn't have been more careful if he'd been operating on the King himself.

The King himself... That was what *he* was.

His role must be vital, Ellie conceded, but part of her was thinking, *What a waste.* To lose the skill those fingers possessed...

'All done,' Marc pronounced. While Ellie had been mostly silent, lost in her own thoughts, he and Chris had been chatting like long-term workmates. Now he took the prepared sutures from Chris and grinned. Procedure done, he had time to relax. 'Want to watch my needlework?' he demanded. 'My mama taught me. If you're going to be a doctor then you learn the basics, she told me, and she had me stitching samplers when boys my age were out playing football. I thought it was sissy.'

'There's nothing sissy about you now,' Chris said soundly and glanced at Ellie. 'I can see why Ellie fell for you.'

'For my needlework? Maybe,' he said and his smile died. 'Not so much for my partner potential.' He went back to concentrating on giving Becky a hairline closure that would hardly mar her bikini line.

And Ellie thought… Ellie thought…

She thought about this town. She thought about her nice, controlled life.

And she thought it was time she got back to not thinking about Marc at all.

With Becky regaining consciousness, with IV and antibiotic lines set up, with Chris and Becky's parents in attendance, there was nothing more for Marc to do. Ellie, on the other hand, had a queue for a now very late afternoon clinic.

She was stressed, she was tired—she'd hardly slept the night before—and she needed to get away from Marc. His presence had her so confused she couldn't think.

'Can I help here too?' he asked.

'Thanks, but I can cope.' She hesitated, knowing she'd sounded brusque. 'But maybe you'd like to collect Felix after school? If you like I can phone his teacher and have him expect you. You can spend a couple of hours telling him about his new future.'

'Thank you,' he said gravely. 'I'd like that.' And then, 'Ellie, I need to go back to Falkenstein tomorrow. Can we have dinner tonight?'

'I do evening surgery on Tuesday.' She glanced at her watch, and he saw her hand suddenly tremble. 'Marc, I'm sorry but I need to go.'

And what was he to say to that?

She was heading back to her medicine.

As mother to the Crown Prince she'd be entitled to a life of luxury. There'd be no need for her to do a thing for the rest of her life except support her son.

He'd tell her that, but he knew already how she'd take it. She'd look at him and return to the medicine she loved.

How jealous was he?

He wouldn't see her again for a month. She was moving out of his life again.

It did his head in.

He'd vowed to take this woman to him, *for as long as we both shall live*. The divorce papers should have negated that, but somehow they hadn't. More than anything in the world he wanted to gather her in his arms and claim her. It felt as if she belonged.

'Goodbye then, Ellie,' he managed and she looked at him calmly, gravely.

'The next few weeks will be hard for you.'

She understood? Of course she did. This woman knew how desperately he'd wanted to be a doctor. And now, instead of the medicine that was a part of him, he was facing the overwhelming responsibilities of head of state. 'They'll be fine,' he managed, even though he knew they'd be hard to the point of unbearable.

'We'll be thinking of you. Me and Felix. Best of luck in learning to be King.'

'I—' He stopped and smiled ruefully. 'Thank you.'

'It can't be harder than first-year internship.' She tried a smile in return. 'The first time you faced a rowdy drunk needing stitches was trial by fire. What could be worse than that? As doctors we've all been there. All else pales.'

'Ellie...' He could hardly get his voice to work.

'You'll do brilliantly,' she said, and then to his astonishment she stepped forward and kissed him. It was a feather touch, a mere brushing of lips on lips, and she pulled away fast before he could respond.

'Best of luck,' she said and she smiled at him. 'You'll make a great king, Your Majesty. See you in Falkenstein.'

CHAPTER SIX

ELLIE HAD BEEN on a plane four times in her life. They'd been short flights to Sydney to attend conferences, sitting in the cheap seats. This flight was different. To say she was nervous would be an understatement.

But Felix wasn't nervous at all. Newly out of his wheelchair, he gloried in this new adventure. He spent hours with his nose glued to the window, explaining to Ellie that Siberia was underneath and he was sure he'd just seen a polar bear. He made friends with everyone. He slept for eight hours in his gorgeous first class bed, his braced leg straight out and safe, and as the plane landed in Falkenstein he was quivering with excitement.

Ellie was quivering too, but it wasn't with excitement.

'Ladies and gentlemen, we're privileged to be carrying members of Falkenstein's royal family on this flight. If you could all please stay seated until they disembark...'

The announcement took her breath away.

Members of the royal family. *Members, plural.*

Felix was still on crutches, but he was clean and brushed and as prince-like as she was able to get him. He might almost qualify as a baby prince.

Ellie was wearing her customary black trousers, white shirt and black jacket. She'd twisted her curls into a knot, as severe as she could make it. *Royal family? Ha!*

'This is nothing to do with me,' she told herself. 'I'll stay in the background.' She took a deep breath, put her hands firmly on Felix's shoulders and led him out of the plane. And in that instant she knew staying in the background would be impossible.

A red carpet lined the steps. A crowd of dignitaries and media was waiting below.

And Marc was there.

The first time she'd seen Marc he'd been wearing a simple suit, shirt and tie. His dark hair had been in need of a cut. He'd just finished med school and that was what he'd looked like. She'd thought he looked gorgeous. But now...

It wasn't fair, Ellie thought, as she blinked in the sunlight, trying to get her head around this new Marc. If she'd seen him like this the first time she'd met him she'd have run a mile.

Because this man was beyond gorgeous.

She knew he'd been part of Falkenstein's army, working as a medic, so she should have expected the uniform, but this was no ordinary uniform. Tassels, gilt, medals...

Oh, for heaven's sake... She wanted to get back into the plane, now.

But Felix had no such reservations. Over the past weeks he'd spent time on the phone to his new-found father. He'd decided he approved, and Marc in uniform clearly met with more of the same.

'Wow! Papa!'

Marc waved and grinned and formality went out of the window. He ran lightly up the plane steps, reached Felix and scooped him off his feet to hug him. Crutches clattered aside, unneeded.

The assembled media went nuts. A hundred-odd cameras were pointed in their direction.

She almost abandoned Felix to his fate. Almost. But this was her baby. She wasn't about to hand him over and run.

Marc was setting him down, holding his shoulders with pride—as if he'd been Felix's father all his life.

Which she supposed he had been, biologically speaking, but still…

And then he smiled at her and she forgot to think of Felix. Who could think of anything past that smile?

'Hey,' he said and his smile was a caress all by itself. 'Ellie. Welcome to Falkenstein. How was the flight?'

'It was awesome,' Felix answered for her. 'I saw a bear and I watched two movies. I had a whole bed and I have a bag full of free stuff. Toothpaste. Earplugs. You want to see?'

'Absolutely,' Marc said, still smiling at Ellie. His smile was a question, though. 'But first, Ellie, I'm sorry but the press got wind of your arrival. Which explains the media, the limousines down there, and my uniform. This is the anticipated arrival of the heir to the throne.'

'You could have warned me,' she muttered. 'I look…'

'You look great.'

'Says the guy with the gold tassels.'

'They come with the job description.'

'I'm a prince now,' Felix interjected importantly. 'Can I have tassels? And medals?'

'Yes to the tassels but you need to earn your medals,' Marc told him. 'Starting now. We need to look royal and wave to the cameras. Ellie…'

'I'll go back inside,' Ellie muttered. 'You two get all the pictures you want. I'm an outsider.'

'You're not,' Marc said gently. 'You're the mother of the heir to the throne of Falkenstein and you'll be accorded all honour. As is your right. Felix, you do need to earn your medals, but your mother should have them pinned to her right now.' And, before she knew what he was about, he took her hand and tugged her around to face the media below. Felix stood before them with Marc's hand on his shoulder. Mother and father and son.

One royal prince in his regimentals. One child who'd one day inherit the throne.

One scared doctor in a suit that needed replacing, with shadows under her eyes from lack of sleep, with all the worry of the world in her heart.

But Marc's arm came around her waist and he smiled at the cameras and there was nothing for it. Ellie smiled too.

She was so far out of her comfort zone she felt as if she might be about to fall off.

The only thing securing her was Marc's arm and that felt dangerous too.

Prince Marc, Crown Prince of Falkenstein. Dr Falken. Her ex-lover and ex-husband.

None of the descriptions seemed to fit. All she knew was that, for now, he was holding her and she needed that hold to steady her.

How had she ever got herself into this mess?

They drove in a limousine to the castle. A sober-faced, dark-suited bodyguard sat beside a uniformed driver. Two dark cars drove front and rear, and armed outriders rode motorbikes beside them.

'Is this necessary?' Ellie managed.

'Royalty comes with a price,' Marc told her. 'Constant security is part of it. But don't worry. For the next few weeks all you need to do is take a holiday. Enjoy yourself.'

'Like that's possible in a million years,' she muttered and then Felix bounced in with information about the flight. He and Marc proceeded to chat about Siberia and bears and an alien movie while Ellie pressed her nose against the window and wondered what she'd got herself into.

The country seemed beautiful. Falkenstein was a tiny kingdom, bordered by massive mountain ranges. The villages they were passing through were full of weathered stone cottages, beautiful churches, quaint shops.

'We have modern centres,' Marc told her, interrupting his conversation with Felix to cut across her thoughts. 'But this approach to the castle is tourist country. We play to it.'

'And why wouldn't you?' she murmured. Then the cavalcade rounded a bend and the palace was just...there.

As if it were hanging in the clouds, it was a fairy tale high on the cliffs, its white stone glistening in the afternoon sun, all turrets and spires and multi-coloured pennants waving gaily in the breeze.

It was vast. It was beautiful.

It took her breath away.

'Wow,' Felix breathed and Ellie thought she couldn't have said better herself. 'Do people really live here?'

'I live here,' Marc said ruefully.

'And do you have servants and butlers and...stuff?'

'Yes, we do.'

'Awesome,' Felix breathed. 'Wait till I tell the guys back home. Do you have horses and swords and dungeons?'

'I believe we do.'

'Wow. Mum, isn't this awesome?'

'Awesome indeed,' Ellie managed and glanced across at Marc.

He was the Crown Prince, complete with tassels and medals and epaulettes and whatever else those decorations on his dress uniform were.

He was smiling with what might even be understanding, but she wasn't in the mood for understanding. No one could possibly know what she was feeling right now.

The only word she could think of was panic.

'If you look down to your left, you'll see a modern red-roofed building beside the river,' Marc told her, and she looked, even though the castle kept drawing her gaze, terrifying the life out of her.

A building with a red roof. Okay, she had it. It seemed to be set in some sort of park leading down to the river.

'That's our local hospital,' Marc told her. 'It's where I've been based for the last six years. Maybe you'd like to see it while you're here.'

'You still have a key?'

He smiled but it was suddenly strained. 'I can go there wherever I want, but I go now as ruling sovereign.'

'Bodyguards included.'

'Bodyguards included.'

'That must suck.'

'It does indeed suck,' he said gravely. 'I miss my job more than I can say. But what I'm doing is more important.'

'Playing dress-up?'

His smile disappeared altogether. He looked down at his beautiful uniform and then he met her gaze head-on.

'If you knew how much I'd rather be in scrubs right now...'

She did know. And with that knowledge part of her panic fell away.

She'd been feeling trapped, but how much more so must Marc feel? She knew how passionate he was about his medicine, yet now he was forced to live in a sugar-frosted fantasy of a palace while the world he loved operated just below him.

'I'm sorry,' she whispered.

His gaze held hers. 'You understand.'

'I guess I do.'

'Thank you,' he said simply. And then his smile returned and her heart twisted as it had no right to twist. *Oh, Marc...*

But her heart had better get itself under control, she told herself harshly.

Marc might be trapped for ever but she wasn't. Four weeks, tops.

It was nine that night before Ellie finally had time to herself.

The day had been crazy, a jumbled mix of introductions, formality and pomp.

She was now in a suite designated for the mother of the heir to the throne. Her bedroom looked the size of a small football field and the attached living room took her breath away. Her meagre luggage had been unpacked by a maid who was more impressively dressed than she was. A woman had arrived and done a quick measure and promised a few outfits 'to make you more comfortable in your surroundings, ma'am.' She was so out of her depth she didn't argue.

Felix was asleep on the other side of the door in an adjoining room. His apartment was similarly impressive. It was set up as a nursery, but not for babies. It was a space most nine-year-olds could only dream of.

There was a nurse sleeping in yet another room, a twinkly lady in her sixties. 'He doesn't need a nurse,' Ellie had stammered when Marc had introduced them and Marc had put a finger to his lips to shush her.

'Hilda was my good, kind nurse when I was a baby. She understands boys and, what's more important, she understands what Felix needs to know. She also has a grandson of about Felix's age. She'll introduce them tomorrow and see if they hit it off. Pierre's English is sketchy but he's bright and fun and Felix might feel better with a friend. Hilda might help you both feel more at home. Now, I'm sorry, Ellie, but I have things I need to attend to. I'll see you later tonight.'

That had been five hours ago. Hilda had taken them on a mind-boggling tour of the palace. She'd answered Felix's thousands of questions. She'd given Felix his dinner and clucked because Ellie wasn't hungry, but finally she'd let Ellie be.

In Ellie's cavernous apartment the silence was deafening.

She peeked through to Felix's room for about the twentieth time. He was in a similar bed, a bed considerably rumpled from having been bounced on. He was fast asleep.

She should be too, but she stood at the great bay window and gazed across the palace gardens to the moonlit mountains beyond and wondered where she'd found herself.

There was a soft knock, as though the person thought she might be asleep.

She was far from asleep, but heaven only knew how much courage it took to open the door.

Marc.

He'd lost the uniform. *Thank heaven for small mercies*, she thought numbly. The uniform alone had been enough to scare her. Now he was dressed in faded jeans and a black T-shirt which stretched tightly across the six-pack of a chest she remembered only too well.

His face was darkened with a five o'clock shadow. It was nine o'clock, she reminded herself, though it didn't feel anything like that. What time was it back in Australia? Who knew?

But she had other things to think about. Marc was here, smiling in concern.

'Hey,' he said softly. 'You should be asleep.'

'I think my body thinks it's seven in the morning.'

'Hilda says you haven't eaten.'

'My body said it was five in the morning when dinner was on offer.'

'So breakfast now?' he asked and looked towards the great bell rope hanging by the mantel.

'Don't you dare,' she said, startled. 'Wake the whole palace because I feel like a toasted cheese sandwich?'

'Is that what you'd like?' His face creased into another smile and it was almost her undoing. Once upon a time she'd fallen in love with that smile.

Whoa. She was not going there again. She was a sensible woman, here to do what had to be done before returning to her sensible life.

If only he wouldn't smile.

'I don't feel like it enough to pull the rope,' she managed. 'Next thing I know there'll be a booming announcement— all staff to the scullery—and I'll be seated at your grand thirty-seater dining table with four footmen and a butler and one cheese sandwich on a silver platter...'

'It is a bit like that,' he said and his smile softened. 'But not quite. The bell pull looks amazing but all it does is light the palace switchboard.'

'Manned by someone who could make booming announcements?'

'I suppose so, but...'

'And the palace cook who's probably just gone to bed would be pulled out to cook again?'

'That's what he's paid for,' he said and then his smile changed again. Suddenly there was a twinkle of mischief lurking within. 'But you know what? I make a mean cheese toastie and I know where the kitchens are.'

'Kitchens?'

'Kitchen,' he said hastily, seeing her look.

She skewered him with a glare. 'How many kitchens?'

'Well, three,' he told her. 'Number one's for everyday use, two's for banquets, three's for State Occasions.'

'So making myself a cheese toastie wouldn't qualify as a State Occasion?'

'It should,' he told her, his smile disappearing. He touched her lightly on the cheek, only a trace, hardly a caress, but it seemed like one to Ellie.

Why? This man was a ghost from her past, nothing more. *Get a grip*, she told herself.

'It should be a State Occasion,' he was saying. 'What you've done for the last ten years, on your own...'

'Is nothing compared with what you've achieved,' she managed. She'd done some intense research over the last weeks and she pretty much had a handle on what his life had been like. 'For your work during the war you're regarded as some sort of superhero. Since then I gather you've been helping run the health system, as well as working behind the scenes, actively politicking so Falkenstein stays peaceful.'

'That's why I need to stay where I am right now,' he told her and his voice turned grim. 'That's why I'm trapped.'

'It's an impressive trap.' Unconsciously her gaze went back to the bell pull and his smile returned.

'It is. To be honest I've pulled that about twice. But come my coronation, with the crown on my head, I imagine I'll be pulling the bell rope like anything. Meanwhile, may I escort you to the smallest of our kitchens and cook you a toastie?'

And what woman could resist a toastie?

What woman could resist that smile?

Not her, she thought helplessly. She was exhausted in every sense of the word. She should close the door on Marc, sink onto the amazing bed and close her eyes on the world.

But a cheese toastie was calling.

And Marc. Prince of the Blood. Her husband.

No, she thought frantically. Not her husband. Just Marc. The father of her son. A man who should be—must be— her friend.

So, it was entirely reasonable to make overtures of friendship. That was what mature couples did in the face of a need for co-parenting.

She could even feel virtuous as he led her out of her room and started the trek through the vast network of portrait-lined galleries and down the back stairs that led eventually to the palace kitchens.

She was doing this for Felix's sake, she told herself. And she was doing this because she was hungry.

She wasn't doing this because Marc made her toes curl at all.

CHAPTER SEVEN

THE 'EVERYDAY' KITCHEN was still grand to the point of intimidating, but Marc was accustomed to cooking for himself. Army messes, campfires, hospital kitchens—he'd learned to ignore his surroundings and get on with it. His French chef might well be miffed that Marc was taking liberties with his frying pan, but for now Marc's focus was on Ellie.

Who sat, pale-faced, worried, watching him as he searched the bank of refrigerators. With increasing frustration.

'Are you sure you wouldn't like a caviar sandwich instead?' he demanded as he found a shelf stocked with smoked salmon and pâté. *Make a note*, he told himself. *Basic Cheddar for toasties needs to be added to the royal shopping list.* He did, however, finally find cheese.

'Pont l'Évêque?' Ellie said faintly, and he grinned.

'Only the best, m'lady. That's all there seems to be.'

'That's all you normally eat?'

'Up until four weeks ago my normal fare's been what's left at the back of the fridge in my apartment. Which isn't pretty. Often it's cheese I've forgotten to wrap. With the furry bits chopped off it makes an awesome sandwich, but obviously tonight we need to slum it.'

'You really had no connection to the royal family?'

'Only as my job dictated. My uncle allowed me to take

over the role of Director of Health after my father died. I've battled with his funding ministers but my uncle never concerned himself directly.'

'So government positions…?'

'Have been assigned purely by whim and favouritism,' he told her, abandoning his search for tomatoes. White asparagus, tick. Tiny designer potatoes? Something that might be kale? Who cooked sandwiches with kale? No tomatoes. *Hmm.* 'My uncle liked the idea that I was family,' he conceded as he searched. 'He seemed to think it gave him more control, but he never bothered to take an interest anyway.'

'Will you?'

He paused. For a long moment he stayed, staring into the fridge as if an answer might magically appear, but then he shrugged and straightened. 'This'll be a toastie with a difference. Hold your hat.'

'Will you?' she asked again.

'Take an interest?' He shrugged. 'I will, but where do I start? Immediately after the coronation I need to sack half the administrators of this country. They've been lining their own pockets for years. It's going to be—'

'Hell?' she finished for him.

'You said it.'

'And your medicine?'

He'd been unwrapping cheese and was about to slice it. Now he closed his eyes as if in pain. 'I can't think,' he said savagely. 'All that training… Never to operate again…'

And he sliced down hard.

Which was a mistake. He stared down in disbelief at the slash on the side of his forefinger.

'Wow,' Ellie said, reaching for the dishcloth. 'Nicely done, Dr Falken. Hold it up. High.' She wrapped the finger tight and propelled it upward and he was left feeling like a king-sized fool.

One large carving knife. One very soft cheese. *What an idiot.*

'Where's the first aid kit?' Ellie demanded, still holding his hand up.

'It's fine. I can…'

'Bleed all over my toastie? I don't think so. I need disinfectant, a couple of Steri-Strips and a bit of gauze. And don't tell me to pull the bell rope. I can deal with this.'

'I can do it myself.'

'Yeah?' A crimson stain was seeping from under the dishcloth. 'Shut up, Marc, and tell me where I can find what I need.'

'There should be a cupboard in the main kitchen with a red cross on it. But—'

'Then don't move. Keep your hand up. Sit and don't faint.'

'I don't faint,' he said, revolted, and she grinned.

'And as a surgeon you don't slice your own finger with a carving knife. It's a whole new world we're living in, Your Highness. Sit down and let me play doctor.'

And for the first time in what seemed like weeks, she felt okay.

Okay? That was a strange word. She was walking through cavernous kitchens looking for a cupboard with a red cross on the front. Marc was in the next room hugging his sliced finger.

Marc was the future King of Falkenstein and she was in a place that did her head in. But, right now, her world had suddenly got domestic.

Marc had a cut finger and she could fix it.

She thought suddenly of how their lives could have been. Rewind the clock. Cancel the war in Falkenstein. Cancel her mother's illness. She and Marc could have stayed married, had their baby, maybe settled down in some nice country practice together. Patched each other's scrapes, supported each other, maybe had a few fights along the way.

Celebrated birthdays, Christmas, wedding anniversaries. Stuff normal couples did.

Ten years later she finally got to put a bandage on a sore finger. *Woo-hoo!*

But for now, suddenly, she was simply grateful for what she could get. Was that stupid? Yes, it was, but it felt okay.

She found the right cupboard and was truly impressed. This wasn't a standard kitchen first aid kit. She needed to move oxygen canisters and a CPR kit out of the way before she could reach what looked like a box of dressings.

There was a dressing for everything. Plus suture material, antiseptic washes and equipment for giving local anaesthetics. This place seemed equipped for everything from childbirth to snakebite.

She fished out an almost embarrassingly large amount of kit and headed back to Marc.

'You want to lie down?' she asked him. 'I have enough dressings to cover you from the toes up.'

'One finger,' he growled. 'I can do it.'

'Like you sliced the cheese? I don't think so.'

'I'm the surgeon.'

'I have a very poor opinion of doctors who have other careers on the side,' she said primly. 'Your carving skills... Being King has obviously messed with your head.'

'Slicing cheese as expensive as Pont l'Évêque messes with my head.'

'Then that's another career you should avoid. You know, it's so soft you could have used a spoon? Hush, Marc, and let me see.'

He cast her a strange look and subsided.

Silence. He sat motionless while she washed his finger, assessed it and decided stitches weren't needed. It'd pull together okay with Steri-Strips. But she needed to get the finger totally dry and apply the Steri-Strips carefully, pulling the sides of the slice together firmly but not rounding the entire finger. It'd swell a bit over the next few hours and if she encased the entire finger, at best it could throb, at worst she'd cut off circulation.

She focused and Marc sat and watched her head bent over his hand—and it felt okay.

To have Ellie treating him.

To have Ellie touching him.

After ten years there should be nothing, he told himself. Or, there again, if there'd been real sexual attraction then there should have been a zing of sheer magnetic pull.

But this reaction was different. Strange.

He was watching the top of her auburn curls. Her attention was absolute. If he cocked his head to the side he could see the tip of her tongue, just emerging, a sign of pure concentration.

He wanted to touch those curls, not for any proprietorial reason, not because he wanted to tug her to him and declare she was still his wife but because he wanted to assure himself she was real.

Their marriage had been so brief, a moment out of time that had seemed almost fantasy. When he'd left her, he'd come home to chaos, war and destruction on an unbelievable level. He'd had to put his head down and work as he'd never worked before and never wished to work again. But at night, lying on the various camp beds in which he'd found himself, he'd often conjured up a vision of Ellie.

Of a life he couldn't have. Of a fantasy.

She'd been that fantasy for almost ten years, his quiet place, a memory that helped him stay steady in times of trouble. Yet here she was, no memory but a woman with premature threads of silver in her hair. A woman with worry lines, put there by a life as demanding as the one he'd faced.

Reality and fantasy were fusing and he didn't know where to take it.

Nowhere at all, he told himself harshly. Ellie's life was back in Australia. Keep your thoughts—and your hands— to yourself, and play the patient.

With the Steri-Strips in place, she was applying gauze dressing. Finally she stepped back, satisfied. 'It should heal fast if you look after it,' she told him. 'It's a sharp knife so the cut's not ragged. Keep it dry and try and keep that dressing intact for a couple of days.'

'Yes, ma'am.'

She cast him an odd look—maybe she was finding this situation as disconcerting as he was—and started clearing up.

'I can do that.'

'Not in my surgery,' she told him. 'And I'm making the toasties now. I might have known a king couldn't cook to save himself.'

'I'm not a king yet.'

'You're surely acting like the coronation's already happened. Pont l'Évêque? I ask you! Maybe I should ask for a frying pan and a fridge in my room so I can cook things normal people eat.'

She was back to being bossy. He remembered Ellie's bossiness. He'd liked it.

With the bench wiped and her hands well washed, she set to inspecting the fridges. There wasn't a lot that met with her approval.

She found bread and butter. She checked the Pont l'Évêque for blood. She set the frying pan on to heat and then glared at the basic supplies.

'You want more than cheese?' he asked.

'We might need to make do.'

'What about using the caviar?'

'Caviar?' She stared at him blankly and then turned to the appropriate fridge. A container of caviar sat on the top shelf, huge and unopened.

'I've never had caviar,' she managed.

'It's good.'

'You have it all the time?'

'Hey, I've been self-funded until now. Caviar hasn't been in my budget. But I have tried it. It might go okay with cheese.'

'You're kidding me, right?'

'A Pont l'Évêque and caviar toastie? Let's try it.'

'Marc…'

But he was grinning. 'You remember those chocolate whisky microwave puddings we invented? We never got around to patenting the recipe. Let's try this as a second invention. Hey, at this rate we could write a cookbook.'

And she flashed a look up at him that was almost fearful.

He could guess why. Memories were everywhere.

Those puddings had been an experiment, made while she was studying and he was in carer mode. The night before her last exam she'd studied to the point where the pages were blurring. He'd made his puddings, lathered them with cream and then fed hers to her, spoon by spoon.

She'd protested and giggled and fed his back to him.

And then they'd made love. The next morning she'd blitzed the exam.

The memory was suddenly so real it almost made him gasp. Ellie was concentrating fiercely on the fridge, then turned back to the table with the tub of caviar, but he knew the same memories were with her. 'Right,' she said in a strained voice and picked up the knife to cut the cheese.

He put his hand over hers. 'Ellie…'

'What?' The look she flashed him was fearful.

'Put the memories aside while you chop the cheese,' he told her. He looked ruefully at his bandaged finger. 'I'm speaking from experience here.'

She looked up. Her gaze met his and held.

He smiled, but for a minute she didn't smile back. She just looked at him, long and hard. As if trying to get him in focus.

And then she sighed and concentrated as ordered on the cheese.

'Right,' she said. 'Chop cheese with care. Ladle caviar without spilling. Fry toasties without burning. I can do this.'

'Of course you can,' he said softly. 'You can do anything.'

They should definitely patent this recipe.

Toasted to perfection, the crusty, golden toasties oozed creamy goodness mixed with golden balls of tang. The sensation was amazing.

While she'd supervised toasting, Marc had foraged in yet another refrigerator and produced a champagne whose label made her jaw drop.

'We can't,' she gasped.

'We have no choice,' he told her. 'My uncle and his family considered this the cheap stuff. In time I'll restock, but for now we're forced to slum it.'

So slum it she did, eating her astounding toastie, savouring the way the caviar burst in her mouth, feeling her tongue tingle with the truly wonderful champagne.

But she was being careful. One glass of bubbles and one glass only.

For this was a night out of frame, she told herself.

For a short few months all those years ago, she'd thought this man could be her soulmate. It was a stupid hope but her heart—and her body—had taken over her sense. She was older now and a whole lot wiser, but this man still made her feel on the verge of something dangerous.

She had herself under control for now—but one glass of champagne was definitely enough.

So she sipped cautiously and she nibbled her toastie and Marc watched her, sort of like the Cheshire Cat watched Alice.

'You're enjoying it,' he said, satisfied.

'You'd better believe it.'

'We can make more. We can open another bottle if we like.'

'You might need to get used to champagne and caviar. I need to go home to Cheddar cheese and soda water.'

'Not on the royal allowance you'll receive,' he said firmly. 'Ellie, whatever course you choose to take, you'll never need to struggle financially again.'

She cast him a fearful look and went back to concentrating on her toastie. There was so much behind that statement. As if she was somehow bound.

Maybe she was. Because of Felix.

No. Two weeks a year here, max, and only then when Felix needed her, she told herself. Her reality was sense. Her little hospital in Borrawong.

But jet lag was making her feel strange, or maybe it was the champagne, or even the crunch from the toastie. The caviar. The setting…

Not the man smiling at her from across the table. Never that.

She finished the last of her toastie and rose. Her champagne was only half drunk. She looked down at it with regret. It was a crime to leave it, and yet the way she was feeling there was no way she was game to take another sip.

'Chicken,' Marc teased and she cast a look at him that clearly displayed her apprehension. Right from the start this man had seemed to be able to read her mind. Once upon a time that had seemed so sexy, so right, so perfect that it set her body on fire.

Now it seemed a threat. This whole situation was a threat.

'Ellie, I won't hurt you,' he told her. 'There's no need to look like that. I understand the terms of this contract. I won't push you further than you wish to go.'

'Why would you want to push me?' She said it almost angrily. She was so far out of her depth.

'I wouldn't. I promise.'

She took a deep breath, trying to move on. 'Marc, what am I going to do for the next few weeks? Hilda's told us the plans for Felix. Introduction to swords and crowns and rings. Meet a friend. Pageantry and fun. It all seems designed to make him want to come back next year. That's okay with me—I understand. But he champs at the bit if I watch. He's learned to be independent and his gammy leg has made that need almost fierce. If he has a friend he'll be better without me.'

'Then take a holiday,' he suggested. 'The palace has three swimming pools. We can organise a chauffeur to take you anywhere you wish. The village has magnificent tourist shopping. I wish I could take you myself but...'

'But you'd be mobbed. And you have other things to do.'

'I do,' he said reluctantly. 'But, Ellie, you need a vacation. Indulge yourself.'

'I don't know how.'

'Learn.'

'I don't think I want to. Marc, isn't there something I can do?'

He hesitated, frowning. She watched his face and there was that recognition again. He knew her. He understood.

It was a jab of knowledge that hurt. It was as if that brief, dry ceremony ten years ago had created a conduit between them, a current of understanding so deep that divorce couldn't break it.

Or maybe it hadn't been the ceremony. Maybe that current had always been there. She thought of the first time she'd seen him, when she'd straightened from the carnage of broken glass and wine and found those dark eyes twinkling at her. That recognition that life could never be the same again.

She was trying to corral her tumbling thoughts, but Marc was still watching her. Did he know what she was thinking now?

She needed an off-switch.

She needed to stay as far away from him as she could for the next four weeks.

'If you'd like a little work…' he said and that helped her steady. Work. That sounded good. She understood the parameters of medicine.

'I guess…the language would be a problem,' he was saying and she thought, *Okay, here goes.* She had to tell him some time.

What would he think? Pathetic? That she'd been clinging to shades of him all this time?

Just say it.

'I don't have a problem with the language,' she told him. 'At least, I don't think I do.'

'What do you mean?'

'I speak your language fluently,' she told him, slipping effortlessly into the lilting Falkenstein dialect that resembled a mix of French, Italian and German, making it relatively simple for Falkenstein's populace to make itself understood all over Europe.

He'd been holding his glass of champagne.

It was all he could do not to drop it.

She sounded as if she'd been born and bred in the streets of Falkenstein.

What the…?

'You taught me some,' she said diffidently, still in his language. 'Just a smattering, but it was enough to get me interested. I got hooked. I bought lessons online and put headphones on as something to do when I needed to relax. And then…' She became even more diffident. 'When Felix was born I started teaching him. I used to sing Falkenstein lullabies to him. How embarrassing is that?'

'Why?' He was staring at her in amazement.

'Who knows?' She tried to talk as if it didn't matter, but she knew she was failing. 'I guess I do know why. I've always felt if you adopt a child from another country you should at least try to let him learn of his background. I thought one day Felix might want to meet you. I know you have brilliant English but who knew? By the time Felix was old enough to travel you might have forgotten.' She grew more tentative. 'Or...or he might wish speak to his half-brothers or sisters. It might...it might make things easier.'

He sounded winded. 'You did this...for me?'

She jutted her chin, almost defiant. 'I'd lied to you about Felix's adoption,' she said. 'You had your reasons for needing to leave us and I understood. This seemed the least I could do. It's no big deal.'

'No big deal! How fluent is Felix?'

'Ask him for yourself. It's a wonder he hasn't already told you, but he's been excited about the surprise and you speak such good English. But he's good.' She smiled, thinking of the indulgence of talking to Felix in a language no one at home understood. It had been like their own secret code.

Now it was a bond to this guy who stood before her.

'So the future Crown Prince of Falkenstein speaks our language,' Marc said, stunned. 'And you didn't tell me.'

'You never asked.'

'I never asked all sorts of things. I never asked how you were. I didn't know your mother died. I simply walked away.'

'Hey, Marc—we had a relationship that lasted exactly five months.'

'Which included marriage.'

'The marriage wasn't real. We closed our eyes to every problem and jumped. It was a fantasy bubble. It burst and that was that.'

'Leaving you holding the baby.'

'Will you cut it out? You talk as if he were a burden. Felix has never been a burden.' She thought of her beautiful boy, sleeping now in his grand apartment. Her boy who looked like his father. 'He's my one true thing,' she whispered. 'My gift. My Felix.'

'I wish I'd shared that.' And it was too much. The tension between them was escalating to the point where they had to touch or run—and running was unthinkable.

Marc reached out and took her hands and held her before him. He didn't say anything. He didn't need to.

She stared down at their linked hands. She was way out of her depth here. She had no idea where her emotions were taking her. She only knew that tugging away was impossible.

'I hate that I haven't had a chance to love Felix,' he said, softly now.

'I know you do, and I'm sorry.'

Silence. There was something building between them. Something so huge.

'Ellie, I did love you,' Marc said at last, as if the words had been forced out.

She turned her gaze to his face. She expected to see confusion. Instead there was wonder.

Admiration?

Intention.

'Marc, no.'

But she knew already what would happen.

She should pull away. She should head straight back to her over-the-top apartment, step through the door and lock it behind her.

'If you really mean no, then I won't touch you,' Marc said and it needed only that. Ever the gentleman. And suddenly she was close to screaming.

What she needed right now was a Neanderthal man, a guy with a club who took all the decisions out of her hands.

Or not?

Neanderthal man might expect a clubbing right back from Dr Ellie Carson. She was no shrinking violet, ready to be carried off at the whim of any man. But then, this wasn't Dr Carson. This was just Ellie, holding hands with Marc.

Or maybe that wasn't the truth either.

Maybe she was still Ellie Falken, the nineteen-year-old who'd met and married this guy out of hand. Who'd fallen in lust at first sight.

Who'd stayed in lust with him all that time?

Only because he hasn't been in your life, she told herself. Her head was screaming advice, trying to make her hormones see sense.

You divorced for a reason, and even if you hadn't divorced, all sorts of other reasons would have reared their heads over time. You've made this man into some sort of fantasy. You're a doctor. You've spent your life working hard, raising Felix, doing the practical things you've needed to do to survive. Be practical now.

But her hormones weren't listening. Her hormones were tilting her chin. Her hormones were raising her feet onto tiptoe but there was no need. Somehow Marc had her by the waist.

Somehow Marc's mouth was claiming hers.

And her body remembered.

The instant surge of heat. The feel of him. The taste, the strength, the sheer animal magnetism. It had blown her away ten years ago and here it was again, fusing their bodies, destroying her defences in an instant. She felt herself whimper as her barriers came down in a cloud of lust. She felt her hands slide up to his face, her fingers glorying in the shape of him, the size of him, the knowledge that this perfect, gorgeous, wonderful man wanted her.

Her.

Had she no sense? She did have sense, she thought dazedly, but right now her sense was a pool of jelly lying uselessly at her feet. Maybe she'd gather it around her again, but not now, not yet. Not while this mouth claimed hers. Not while his arms held her against him, while her breasts were crushed against his chest, while her mouth tasted him, savoured him, owned him.

There was no future for her here. She had enough sense to know it, but surely there was no harm in kissing.

And it wasn't as if she had a choice. He was kissing and she was kissing back, and if World War Three erupted around them right now she wouldn't notice. All she wanted was this man.

He could take her, she thought wildly. Right here. Her hands were tugging him closer. She wanted him more than life itself.

Ten long years. Her body remembered and screamed that this was what she'd been missing for all these years and she'd blocked it out, but it had never properly disappeared.

This man. Her husband.

'Ellie…' Somehow he tugged back, just a little. He was holding her face now, cupping her chin, looking down at her with an expression she'd never seen before.

'Marc…'

'You are my wife.'

She wasn't. The sensible part of her shouted it. She'd never been a wife to this man, the Crown Prince of Falkenstein. She'd been wife to just-qualified Dr Marc Falken, a friend, a colleague, a guy who'd been a little bit older but almost equal.

But now wasn't the time to say it. Not now, not when her body was making demands she had no hope of denying.

'Enough of the complications,' she managed. 'Just kiss me.'

He wanted her as he'd never wanted anything or anyone in his life before. She felt like his.

She was his.

He'd had relationships over the last ten years—of course he had. He was a divorcee but most women didn't hold that against him. One failed marriage didn't mean a life of celibacy.

And yet that one sweet time had messed things for him. No one felt the same as Ellie. No one moved him as Ellie did.

He'd told himself what he'd had with Ellie had been his first real passion. That if it had been allowed to run its course, with luck it would have mellowed into the day-to-day fondness and friction he assumed most marriages became. It was simply that he'd been wrenched away before that initial passion had dried up, meaning it had messed with his head for years.

So there was no reason why that passion should flare as it did now. There was no reason his body should respond as if this was his place, his right. As if Ellie was part of him and he was part of her.

How could a marriage vow do this? It couldn't.

Fate, duty, lawyers had separated them for sensible reasons. So why was his heart feeling as if it might burst in his chest with the joy of holding her?

Ellie...

His love. His wife.

But, even as he thought it, the door opened behind them. And Ellie pulled back as if she'd been struck.

The look of bliss, the look he'd remembered and loved, was suddenly replaced by distress.

Which was matched by the men at the door, two security guards with horror written clearly on their faces as they recognised what—and who—they were interrupting. 'Your Highness... So sorry... The motion sensors— Uh... the camera angle was blocked by the fridge door, so we were asked to check. If we'd known... A million apologies. A million...' And they backed out as if they expected the firing squad to follow.

Leaving Ellie staring at Marc as if he was part of the same firing squad.

'Love, Ellie, don't…'

'I'm not your love.' It was a fierce whisper.

'No.' He took a deep breath. 'But you could be.'

'Not any more. You walked away.'

The security guards were forgotten. What was between them was too overwhelming to admit thoughts of anything else.

All he wanted to do was step forward and take her into his arms again, but the fear on her face stopped him dead.

'I did walk out on you,' he said, somehow managing to make his voice calm, maybe even reasonable. 'Ellie, I didn't have a choice. And you didn't follow.'

One accusation was now two.

'You knew I couldn't.'

'I know that. We had no choice.'

'But if we'd really loved each other…' Her voice cracked. 'I know. The whole thing was impossible but it still felt… mad. Wrong. That you were suddenly in the midst of war on one side of the world and I was coping with my mother's illness and a fraught pregnancy on the other. But we were married, Marc. Married! It was a mockery and it hurt like you wouldn't believe. Do you think I'd want to put myself through that again? Leave me be, Marc Falken. Your Majesty. Whoever you are. I don't care who you are. All I know is that you're not my husband. You never were and you never can be.'

'We could—'

'We couldn't,' she said flatly. 'Marriage is for ever and we can't do for ever. It's not our fault, but we can't. Leave it, Marc. Thank you for the toastie. I'm going to bed.'

There didn't seem to be anything left to say.

She walked to the door and then turned. 'Marc?'

'Mmm?' He was feeling kicked. Winded. Blasted by the surge of raw emotion that had washed through his body, leaving him gutted at the end of it.

'We're here for four weeks. I need a job. You implied I might be able to work.'

'You need a holiday. There are swimming pools, a gym, a library loaded with English books as well as books in our language...'

'Holidays do my head in,' she said shortly. 'I need to stay busy. That hospital—could I do something? Even hospital visiting or helping in rehab, something to take my head out of where it's at.'

And he got it. He knew what she was saying because he felt the same.

The tension was tangible. Inescapable. The only thing to do was escape.

Into medicine? Wasn't that what he longed to do also?

'I'll make enquiries,' he told her. 'If possible, I'll take you over the hospital tomorrow afternoon.'

'Thank you, but I don't need an escort.'

'Give me that honour, please.'

'Marc...'

'Yes?'

'What's between us is too complicated for words,' she whispered. 'Please, don't make it any harder.'

CHAPTER EIGHT

How was a person supposed to sleep in a cloud of feather comforters, silk sheets and velvet hangings? In a room where windows opened to a view to the mountains beyond, where peacocks roamed in the foreground, where generations of royals led their pampered existence—and she was now one of them?

But not really.

She was the wrong actress for this set. She slept fitfully and woke feeling just as discombobulated.

Felix, however, had none of her qualms. The moment he woke he limped through to join her.

'Isn't this awesome? I can bounce and bounce on my bed and Hilda says I'm a prince so if I want to bounce then it's okay.' He climbed on her bed and prepared to demonstrate.

She edged sideways fast. 'Felix, crutches, floor.'

'I'm the boss of the world. I should be able to take my crutches anywhere.'

'You're not the boss of your mum or your mum's bed.'

'No, but I'm important.'

'For four weeks, Felix, and then we go home.'

His face fell. 'I don't think I want to.'

'Can I come in?'

Marc.

Felix whooped. 'Of course! Hooray! Mum, it's Papa.'

Great. The memory of the night before was all around

her. Ellie wanted to pull up the covers and disappear, but Felix was grinning a welcome and shifting on the bed. 'Come in. This is a pyjama party.'

Except Ellie wasn't wearing pyjamas. Her nightgown was awful and her hair was a bird's nest and she felt...as if she didn't belong here.

'Is it okay with you, Ellie?' Marc was still at the door, waiting for her to speak. 'I'm not in pyjamas.'

He wasn't. He was in jeans and a T-shirt and he looked almost normal. Except there was nothing normal about this man.

Talk about sex on legs!

Um...maybe that was a really dangerous thing to think.

'I didn't want to wake you,' he told her, coming further into the room. 'But Hilda said Felix had bounced in here.'

'Bounced being the operative word.'

'You sound bitter.'

'Really?' She glowered at her son. 'Why would that be? Surely I like being hit on the nose with crutches at the crack of dawn.'

Marc chuckled and her heart did that crazy lurch again. *Oh, for heaven's sake...*

But Marc, at least, was moving on. 'Felix, have you ever ridden a horse?'

'No.' Felix was suddenly glowering. 'I can't even ride a bike now. My legs...'

'Have been all over the place,' Marc said, matter-of-factly. 'With one leg shorter than the other, it must have been hard. But your mum sent me your medical history and the doctors' notes on your last operation. Your legs should be fine with some physical therapy.'

'But I'm still on crutches.'

'Crutches won't stop you learning to ride.' He hesitated. 'Felix, for the coronation it's usual for the King to ride. Your leg will still be in a brace, but if you could learn to keep your seat...' He grinned. 'I know you'd rather ride in a Baby Austin, but royal tradition doesn't stretch that far. It would be excellent if you rode with me. What do you think?'

'R…ride?' Felix stammered. 'Cool!'

Marc grinned. 'Brave kid. But there's not much to it. We'll give you lessons. We'll find you a quiet horse and you and your mum can ride together.'

'I don't ride.' It was a desperate snap and in fact it was a lie. Her grandfather had taught her as a child but the thought of riding beside her son—and Marc—in a coronation parade was overwhelming.

'You should learn too,' Marc told her. 'I'll teach you.'

'It's not that I can't ride. It's that I don't—and I don't need you to teach me!'

'Mum!' Felix stared in astonishment. 'You should be polite.'

She chewed her lip and glared at Marc, but he only smiled at her. He knew what he was doing. That twinkle…

This man was so dangerous.

'It's okay, Ellie. I'm not dragging you into the royal family.' The twinkle deepened. 'The opposite, in fact. I've talked to the director of the hospital and organised to take you for a tour. Felix, if you're happy doing your riding lesson without me, our chief groom, Louis, has taught more kids to ride than you've had hot dinners. The brace on your leg will protect it and the mare we have in mind won't let a brace worry her.' His smile widened. 'Louis doesn't speak English but your mum says that won't be a problem for you.'

'I didn't realise it was your language Mum taught me until yesterday,' Felix said, indignant. 'She never told me why we were learning.'

'That's my fault,' he said, suddenly grave. 'Your mum did it as a surprise for me, and it's wonderful. So, would you like to ride a horse?'

'If he's careful,' Ellie said, feeling desperate. 'If he falls…'

'We'll take care. Ellie, you know I'd never suggest it if it could do harm.'

'You think teaching him he's boss of the world won't do harm? He even says he's now allowed to bounce on his bed.'

And Marc laughed again, that lovely deep chuckle that made her heart twist and twist again.

'What kid doesn't bounce on his bed?' he demanded.

And Ellie thought of the narrow bed Felix slept in at home—and the deep sag in the middle. She had to smile back.

That was a mistake. Her smile faded and so did Marc's. *Oh, help.*

She could so easily fall.

She'd fallen so hard, so fast, last time, but she hadn't considered the consequences.

Ten years on, she was no longer a green girl, falling into lust with a handsome prince. She gave herself a good mental shake, and seemingly so did he.

'I have a meeting now,' he told her, glancing at his watch, suddenly businesslike. 'But if you can be ready at ten we'll go to the hospital together.'

'I can go by myself. There's no need...'

'There is a need,' he said, suddenly fierce. 'This job takes up ninety per cent of my time. Allow me to choose what I do with the rest.'

'You want to go to the hospital?'

'I'm a surgeon. What do you think? If I can't take my wife...'

'I'm not your wife.'

'No.' He sighed. 'You're not. And I'm no longer a surgeon. But grant me this indulgence, Ellie. I'll take you to the hospital and introduce you to the world I've left behind.'

'Marc...'

'Ten,' he said harshly. 'Yes?'

'Yes,' she said because there was nothing else to say.

Because she was suddenly seeing a pain as great as any she'd seen as a doctor, and it was a pain she could do nothing about.

The hospital was a short walk down from the fortified cliffs that formed the first part of the palace wall. The path crossed the river and then meandered through the cobbled streets of the old part of the town. The day was beautiful. Ellie was itching for a walk—but a limousine was waiting in the palace courtyard. A royal flag was mounted on the car's bonnet. A uniformed chauffeur was holding the door wide and four outriders were mounted on huge black motorbikes.

Marc was dressed in a suit now and his face was set. He'd met her inside but hardly spoken.

The chauffeur ushered them into the car and closed the door behind them. A glass panel between driver and passengers gave them privacy. The big car purred out from the palace grounds, their motorbike escort riding in perfect symmetry.

People paused as they passed. The younger generation stared. Older people bowed or curtsied.

'Get this,' Ellie breathed. 'It's like something out of a fairy tale.'

'Or a nightmare,' Marc muttered and then they were at the hospital and there was a reception committee lined up to receive them. The hospital director. The head of medicine. The head of surgery. The charge nurse.

Marc had had responsibility for the healthcare system of the country, Ellie knew, but he'd also worked here as a surgeon. These people would have considered him a colleague. Now they were reacting to him with deference, even a little fear.

She could sense his tension and she knew he hated it.

For the director was showing them through the hospital as if Marc hadn't seen it before. They were ushered from ward to ward, the director giving an efficient over-view. Every ward was beautifully ordered. Even the patients looked neat. Patients and nursing staff were looking on with deference but also, Ellie sensed, with concealed impatience. This formal visit was an interruption in their day. They had things to do.

The last place they were ushered was Emergency. Here, too, the place was clinically clean, cubicles pristine and ready to receive anyone needing assistance. But there seemed little need. Nurses in each occupied cubicle tended patients whose care looked well under control but only half the cubicles were full. The young doctor in charge—*very* young—greeted them with what seemed strained formality.

The director was talking hard at Marc, boasting of efficiency, but the place didn't seem normal. What emergency department in the world ever looked like this? And Marc was frowning at the director, eyeing the ward with disbelief.

On impulse she edged to the door leading to the ambulance bay.

There were five ambulances lined up outside.

'Do you have patients waiting to be admitted?' she asked.

'Everything is under control,' the young doctor said, with a nervous glance at the director.

'Really?' But Marc must have been sensing exactly what Ellie was feeling—maybe more so, because he'd worked here before. Until now he seemed to have been holding himself in rigid control. Now that control seemed to snap. He stalked over to Ellie so he, too, could see the waiting ambulances, then turned back to the director. 'I didn't come here expecting to see a pretty hospital,' he snapped. 'What is this? You've directed the ambulances not to unload until we're gone?' He turned to the young doctor, ignoring the director. 'Why?' And the force of his question demanded the truth.

'Because royalty's not supposed to see this place when it's under stress,' the young doctor said, sounding desperate. 'You know that, sir... Your Highness. We don't have enough doctors—you know that too. I'm the only one on duty this morning. Yes, we have patients lined up and as soon as you leave it'll be hell. But for now we're ready for inspection, as requested.' And the look he cast at the director was one of pure defiance.

'Stefan?' Marc growled, staring at the director and the director spread his hands.

'We were given a directive from the palace,' he said simply. 'We were to expect a royal visit with overseas dignitaries. The rule is never to lose face.'

'And lose lives instead?' Marc's face was like thunder. He glanced at Ellie and then shrugged. 'Sorry, Ellie, I guess you're the overseas dignitary but the tour stops now.' He tugged off his jacket and tie and tossed them onto the admissions desk. 'Right. Let's get them in.'

The director stared at him as if he were from another planet. 'Sir... Your Highness, it's not fitting...'

'Of course it's fitting,' Marc growled. 'Those are my people out there. Ellie, I'll have someone escort you back to the palace.'

'Are you kidding?' For the first time since she'd arrived Ellie felt a surge of belonging. Ambulances filled with need were her stock-in-trade. 'If I'm allowed to work here...' She turned to the director. 'I have current Australian medical registration. Will your insurance cover me if I start work now?'

The man looked like a goldfish, mouth open, eyes boggling. His royal tour had just been turned on its head.

'Of course it will,' Marc snapped. 'One phone call... Stefan, go make it. Dr Eleanor Carson, Australian Medical Practitioner, has just joined your staff, starting now.'

* * *

The administrators disappeared. The emergency room filled and Ellie put her head down and went for it.

She blessed the fact that she spoke the language. She had minor hiccups—the language tapes she'd worked on hadn't foreseen convoluted explanations such as: *I tripped over the kid's skateboard and stuck my arm with a tray of satay skewers...* Or: *I have a bit of pain in my gut and the wife fusses—but it's her bloody fish bake that did it...*

But she had enough vocabulary to get by, and the nurses were great. They were ready to speak slowly or translate into English.

And Marc was just across the room.

He was handling the serious stuff. A woman arrested just as they brought her in—what had they been thinking to leave someone with severe chest pain waiting in an ambulance? The young doctor—a couple of years out of med school at most, Ellie thought—deferred to Marc with obvious relief. Together they managed to get a heartbeat. Then Marc barked the demand to call in a cardiac specialist.

But the young doctor was hesitant. 'He's not on call except for emergencies,' he quavered and Marc stared at him in incredulity.

'What exactly do you think qualifies as an emergency? Ring him now!'

Ellie looked through at the woman's husband, wringing his hands through the glass door leading to the waiting room. He was covered with dust from what looked like mining or some other equally filthy task and she also wondered what qualified as an emergency if not a cardiac arrest.

And why were they so short-staffed?

But now wasn't the time to discuss staffing issues. She had the dad with the arm pierced with skewers to cope with and Marc was moving on to a toddler with a burned hand.

They had their triage worked out. Somehow they'd become a team, figuring what the young doctor was capable of, filling the gaps, working around him, with him, for him.

Who knew what Marc had scheduled for the rest of the day? For now it didn't matter.

At one stage Josef appeared, looking frantic, but another ambulance had just rolled up and Marc waved him away with a snap.

'Nothing's more important than this. Reschedule. Oh, and let Felix know where his mother is. Hilda will make sure he's okay.'

Josef looked at Marc's grim face and disappeared without a word.

They worked on. The place settled into the normal chaos of an emergency ward, with the three doctors working together, doing what they did best.

It felt okay.

Who needed a holiday? Ellie thought as the morning became afternoon. This felt great.

But why did this feel so different than at home?

And she glanced at the young doctor, Luc. He was discussing ongoing care with Marc, deferring to Marc as the senior doctor. Now he looked competent, intelligent, decisive, but he'd looked strained to the point of breaking when they'd walked in. She could only imagine the orders that had come from above. *Royal visit—clear the area and make it look pristine and under control.* He didn't look old enough or assured enough to defy such an order. What was such a young doctor doing in charge of a department as busy as this?

And to be alone, as she was alone at home...

The afternoon Marc had arrived she'd been faced with a carload of injured teens and she'd been terrified. She'd had too much work and every decision had been hers. She watched Luc now, discussing the current case with Marc, and she realised loneliness had many guises.

She was going home to more of the same.

What was she doing, thinking she was lonely when she had a community to envelop her? She could remarry. A couple of the local farmers had made it clear they were interested.

Why had she never been interested in them?

'Will I be okay?' The elderly lady she'd been treating quavered her question and Ellie's attention jerked back to where it should be. The woman had fallen and jarred her hip, but the X-ray had shown no break.

'You'll be more than okay,' she told the woman in her own language. 'But you've been lucky. You need handrails on those steps straight away.'

'I'm on a list,' the woman told her. She nodded towards Marc, who was treating a young girl who'd burned herself trying to wax her own legs. The girl had arrived feeling frightened and embarrassed, and then she was stunned to silence when her treating doctor turned out to be the new King. But Marc now had her laughing. He was telling her a silly story about his first ever attempt to shave. True or not, it had the girl relaxed. Smiling. Adoring.

The woman Ellie was treating had exactly the same worshipful look on her face, and suddenly Ellie realised she did too.

Oh, for heaven's sake...

'They say he'll change things,' the woman told her. 'They say hospital waiting lists will go down and schools will get more money. But there's so much work for him to do. I can't understand why he's here.'

'I guess he's needed here now,' Ellie told her.

'He's needed everywhere.'

'Then let's play our part and get that scrape cleaned so your daughter can take you home,' Ellie said, with a last glance across at Marc. He had so much on his plate. So much responsibility, but his sole intent now seemed to be making one teenager smile.

He was needed everywhere and he knew it. And so did she.

Marc worked through until three. He spoke again to the director—who just happened to keep checking in—and at change of shift two doctors appeared instead of one.

'It'll blow my budget,' the director fussed but Marc shrugged.

'Wear the loss until after the coronation. The budget of the entire country is about to be rewritten.'

And that could be the rest of my life right there, he thought grimly, envisaging the budget calculations, foreseeing hour upon hour of endless negotiations with so many needs.

The country's funding had been skewed for years towards indulging royal whims. Marc himself had fought for medical funding. He could grant that now, but there was desperate need in education, housing, welfare, infrastructure... So many things. But for now he'd worked for five hours beside Ellie and it felt good.

He needed to return to the palace. Ellie needed to return to Felix. They both wanted a walk.

He said as much and his security people stared at him as if he'd grown two heads.

Walking home was what people did every day, yet it turned out to be an undertaking so extraordinary Marc almost gave up.

But he was the new King. Surely the title had to be good for something. 'Deal with it,' he growled and led Ellie out into the sunshine.

His outriders were still there, patiently waiting. Here was a cost saving he could make, he thought, and he attempted to wave them away. But his chief of security was having kittens, so a compromise was reached. He and Ellie walked but they had bodyguards walking before and after.

Five minutes after they left the hospital a helicopter appeared and hovered overhead.

And Ellie got the giggles. 'I feel like an ocean liner with tug boats,' she told him. 'So much for our peaceful stroll. What do you think a chopper could do if I attacked you with the secret knife inside my left shoe? Drop a bomb?'

'They're not worried about you.'

'Then what are they worried about?'

'The royal family's made themselves amazingly unpopular.'

'But you're going to fix that, right?' she said and she suddenly tucked her arm into his. It was a gesture of friendship, nothing more, he told himself, but it felt…great. 'You started today. The patients you treated loved you.'

'Only one I treated was able to talk!'

'Yeah, well, she loved you. Swapping shaving stories—I can't think of any better way to win adoration.'

He chuckled and the mood, blackened with the fuss made by security, lightened immeasurably. They were approaching the ancient bridge over the river. The castle was beyond, a fairy tale of turrets and shimmering stonework. The sun was shining and the river was shimmering and calm.

He had a sudden urge to highjack one of the boats beneath them and leave. Go where the river took him.

'You need to figure out a way to keep your medicine,' Ellie told him and his mind jerked from fantasy back to reality.

'You think I can do this every day? Have you any idea how many appointments were set aside because—?'

'Because you saved lives? Which is what you want to do.'

'You know more than anyone we can't always do what we want.'

'No,' she said softly, and her hand suddenly slipped into his. Naturally, as if it had the right to be there. 'But how often do you have to give in?'

'Is that you asking? The Ellie who wanted to be a neurologist? The Ellie who's now a country doctor, working in a place she vowed never to return to?'

Silence. He hadn't meant to sound angry. He hadn't meant to sound frustrated. But both of those things were obvious. The afternoon was still. Sound carried and the bodyguards glanced in astonishment before regaining their impassive demeanour.

'There must be some way.' Ellie didn't seem to have heard his anger. Her hand was still tucked in his, as if he hadn't just tried to hurt her. 'Marc, you can't spend the rest of your life sitting in your oval office being King. You're not that sort of guy.'

'It's not oval.'

'I bet it's big.'

'It is big.'

'And scary?'

'And scary,' he admitted.

'And I've seen the films of the Queen. Do you have red boxes too?'

'Gold boxes.'

'Oh, of course. Gold.' She nodded. 'Important, huh?'

'Very important.'

'All of it?'

'I'm not supposed to discuss…'

'Of course you're not. So you're not discussing. Just nodding. All of it important?'

He said nothing. They were approaching the far end of the bridge but their steps slowed. There were things to be sorted before they entered the intimidating walls of the palace.

'So a secretary could maybe sort the boxes and mark

the important stuff?' Ellie tried cautiously. 'That could give you time.'

'Who could I trust to tell me what's important? That's what my uncle did—left the decisions to minions. As long as the royal family got what they wanted, they were happy.'

'You're not that sort of King.' She hesitated. 'But, Marc, you've given up so much already.'

'Our marriage, you mean? Our son?'

And there it was, out in the open.

They stopped. The security guys edged closer. Marc waved them back, out of earshot.

'Very imperious,' Ellie commented and Marc glowered.

'No, I meant it as a compliment,' Ellie told him. 'Is that what Felix will be doing for the next few weeks? Going to Imperious School?'

'Ellie…'

'You did give up Felix for your country,' she said softly. 'You did give up our marriage.'

'If I remember correctly, you did the same. You made the decision to care for your mother and to put our son up for adoption.'

'There didn't seem a choice,' she whispered. 'But, Marc, if we'd really tried…'

'How could we have tried any harder?'

'Maybe by honouring the vows we made? Maybe by at least staying in contact. I don't know. It all seemed impossible at the time, just as your decision to take on the throne to the exclusion of everything else seems the only option now. But surely—'

'Surely nothing. There is no choice.'

'So you'll sit in your grand office and play with gold boxes and live happily ever after.'

'Don't belittle what I'm trying to do.'

'I can't. Nor can I judge. I made decisions too, Marc. All I know is that my decision ten years ago, to abandon you—' she caught herself '—to abandon our son was the wrong one. Thankfully, I could reverse it. But your decision now to walk away from medicine...'

But his attention was no longer on his choice. It was on her words. 'Your decision to walk away from me was wrong? What are you saying...?'

'We were kids,' she managed. 'What's done can't be undone. But it made us...it made me unhappy, and seeing you today, seeing you do what you do best, but knowing you need to walk away again...it's breaking my heart. Marc, I know you need to take the throne but to walk away from your medicine seems equally impossible. You're needed.'

'I can organise funds for more doctors. As ruler I can make things better.'

'Of course, but maybe you can do that in the afternoons and in the morning you can take out the odd appendix.'

'With my security guards at the ready.'

'They'd be just as bored watching you work through boxes, and this way they can flirt with the nurses. Surely you can do a few sessions a week. And hey, it'll keep your hand in. If the peasants revolt then you can go back to work.'

'My job is to stop the peasants revolting.'

'Which is much more likely if your people see you care. What you did today...'

'Ellie, you can't tell me how to run my life. What about yours? Are you planning to bury yourself in Borrawong for the rest of your life?'

Silence. They should keep going, Marc thought grimly. Officials would be waiting. Boxes would be waiting.

The rest of his life was waiting.

He turned again to the river. House martins were swooping under the parapets, in and out of the shadows. A dragonfly flittered past. Two birds dived with precision, carrying their unfortunate victim triumphantly towards land.

He felt like the dragonfly. Caught.

And then he thought, *The birds worked as a team.*

A team...

'Ellie?'

'Mmm?'

'Stay with me.'

Silence.

'What...?' she managed at last. 'What do you mean?'

He hardly knew himself. He hadn't meant to say it but it was out there, demanding a continuation.

He didn't turn to look at her. He couldn't. But what needed to be said had to be said.

'You still feel like my wife.'

Her breath hissed in so sharply it hurt. 'That's...that's nonsense. We've been divorced for nine years.'

'Then why does it still feel as if we're married?'

'It doesn't.'

'Liar. Last night—'

'Was only a kiss. It didn't mean—'

'It was more than a kiss.' He hesitated. This wasn't the time or place to say it, but his thoughts were so huge, so urgent they had to find words. The bodyguards had backed off a little. They almost had privacy.

'Ellie, when we separated we broke each other's hearts,' he said, feeling his way through each word. 'You've said as much. I've never remarried and that's been for a reason. I've always felt married. Seeing you again...nothing's changed. It still feels like you're my wife. If you feel the same...why not remarry? Bring Felix up together. Share our lives again.'

She turned and stared at him in incredulity. 'What are you saying?'

'You heard,' he said evenly. 'Ellie, it makes sense. To share our lives...'

'Again. That's what I thought you said. Are you kidding? We never shared our lives.' Her voice was almost a yell. She'd forgotten the bodyguards; she was too shocked, too angry to consider. 'We were together for mere months, for not much longer than one long vacation. My life was Borrawong, my community, my mum. Your life was your country. We met and forgot everything we should have remembered. You weren't even truthful about who you were. So sharing our lives again? You're saying now that we could pick up pieces that didn't exist in the first place?'

This was impossible. How much would he give to be able to step forward now, take her into his arms, tell her how much she was loved? That he'd never stopped loving her. That walking away from her had killed something in him that he'd thought was gone for ever.

But she was looking at him as if he was crazy, and maybe he was. What had she said? *One long vacation...* Maybe that was all their marriage had been, yet what havoc it had wrought in their lives! And here he was again, suggesting an even greater upheaval.

What right did he have? None, he thought grimly, but he thought again of the advantages and knew he needed to press on.

'Ellie, it could be sensible. Setting aside the attraction we feel for each other...'

'Yeah, let's set that aside. It scares me stupid.'

'Okay.' He held up his hands as if in surrender. 'But I would like some say in Felix's upbringing. I would like to share him. And yes, that's all about me, but for you... Ellie, you could have fun. Felix could be brought up here, knowing the palace, knowing his people and you could do what you like. Work as a doctor if you wish. Relax and do nothing if you wish that more.'

'Lie beside one of your over-the-top pools and sip drinks with little umbrellas.' She was still staring at him as if he had two heads. Or as if he frightened her, which was far, far worse.

He was struggling to hold it together, to sound practical rather than emotional. To take that look of fear away.

'That's what the women of this family have done from time immemorial.'

'Gee, thanks. I don't think so.'

'Ellie, ten years ago I came home because there was no choice,' he tried. 'You stayed with your mother because there was no choice. But you have a choice now.'

'But you still don't,' she said flatly.

And he didn't. 'The throne is non-negotiable,' he agreed. He paused, fighting his own anger and frustration. Fighting to make this proposition sound logical. 'I know it's a huge ask, but it might just work. I could offer you my support and protection, things you should have had for the last ten years. I can help with Felix. Felix would have a father as well as a mother and you know he'd enjoy that. What do we have to lose? And it'd make it so much easier…'

'For you.'

'Yes.' What else could he say but the truth? 'But for you too. And for Felix as well.'

'Leave us out of it. What are you proposing—that I marry you again so you'll have more time for your boxes?'

'I didn't mean that.'

'So what did you mean?'

'I mean I've never considered us not married.'

She shook her head in disbelief. 'You're kidding. Nine years…'

'I'm not saying I've been faithful.' He was fighting to explain something he barely understood himself. 'But all these years… Ellie, our divorce was supposed to nullify our vows but it didn't work. Not for me. I've never imagined marrying someone else. I knew I never could.'

'Because the country would call? Because imperatives would win and marriage would be put aside again?'

'You sound bitter.'

'Why would I be bitter? Haven't I had long enough to get over it?' She shrugged. 'Of course I have, but for me, like you, it's left scars. We married in passion, but that passion

wasn't enough to hold us together. So it broke my heart.
And, yes, I was only nineteen and having a broken heart
is what all nineteen-year-olds are expected to experience,
but it hurt so much I learned never to go down that path
again. You say you haven't been chaste. You haven't held
our marriage vows sacred after divorce. Well, neither have
I, but the men I've dated have been sensible.'

'Sensible?'

'What's wrong with sensible? Sensible's safe. Sensible
doesn't leave me whimpering under the covers at three in
the morning.'

'Ellie...'

'And don't you feel sorry for me. I didn't whimper for
long,' she snapped. 'I'm over it. I'm over you. Marc, I know
you'll make this country a better place because that's your
role. But for me to stay here and play part-time wife when
you have a few moments to spare... Marc, that might just
break my heart all over again.'

She met his gaze with defiance.

But he saw through it. She still looked tired. Worried.
And afraid. He wished she could have rested instead of
working this morning. If she was his wife he could insist...

Insist? Who was he kidding? She was strong, feisty, determined, a country doctor from Australia. He had no right
to demand she give that up.

He couldn't demand. He couldn't even ask.

'Leave it,' she was saying, and she sounded infinitely
tired. 'Just leave it, Marc. Coming here was a mistake. It
was hard for both of us but let's not make things worse.
I'll stay as I promised, but as soon as the coronation's over
I'll take Felix home.' She hesitated, closing her eyes for a
minute. When she spoke again it seemed she was struggling to find the right words.

'Marc, you walked away from me nine years ago. I don't
blame you, because I walked away from you as well. But,
no matter whose fault it was, no matter how stupid we were

for marrying in the first place, after nine years I've pulled myself together. Felix has been a big part of that, the part I didn't walk away from. I can't walk away from him and I won't, but neither will I let myself lose control again.'

Then she took a deep breath and faced him head-on.

'Enough. Forget the marrying bit. It's forgotten. Over. But, Marc…you know what else I didn't walk away from? My medicine. I'm a doctor. Even today, discombobulated as I am, medicine settles me and I know it does you too. It's what we trained for; it's what we are. But here you are, walking away again.'

'I have no choice!'

'Exactly. You know, if I was stupid enough to agree to marry you again, to be part of this goldfish bowl, who's to say someone won't come to me in the future and say it's not safe, it's not proper, the people don't want me to be both Queen and doctor. What if they say I have responsibilities to the palace and I need to give up medicine? Like they're saying to you.'

'It won't happen.' But he felt ill. Her words were battering, and he couldn't defend himself because everything she said was true.

'Marc, all those years ago you suggested I might follow you out here, play the little wife, only you said don't come until the war's over because it'll be dangerous. You had important work to do and you couldn't be worrying about me while you did it. But you never once asked me to share your burden. And I had Mum and my responsibilities and I didn't ask you to share my burden either. So I stayed independent. But you know what? I've loathed bringing my son up not knowing his father. And I loathe the fact that I still love you!'

'You still…?'

But she held up her hands, as if to fend him off. 'Don't go there,' she said wearily. 'Because my loving you now feels like some sort of internal blackmail and I won't listen.

I need to go home. Marc, if you need a consort, find some-one sensible. Find someone who'll enjoy this life, who'll keep your bed warm when you have time to join her. Who won't be hurt when you leave her. You need to be sensible.'

'But if you love me...isn't that cowardice?'

And she lost it. 'Back off!' she yelled and then, as Marc's bodyguard took a synchronised, instinctive step forward, she grimaced and lowered her voice. 'Thinking we were in love wasn't enough to save our marriage nine years ago and, with the stress you're under, how can it be any different now? Forget this conversation, Your Highness. From now on our dealings need to be strictly official, starting now. This conversation is finished because, from this moment on, I'm being sensible for both of us.'

CHAPTER NINE

ELLIE DIDN'T SEE Marc for the rest of the day. 'His Highness is needed for state matters. He sends his apologies,' Josef told her that night and she felt vindicated.

She also felt sick. She was right but there was no joy down that road.

Marc wanted her, but he wanted her on his terms, or terms decreed by this appalling job, and how could she reconcile the two?

'When do you think we'll see him again?' Felix demanded as she tucked him in that night. She thought of all the years she'd tucked Felix in alone and she felt her chest clench in pain.

She should never have agreed to come. It hurt so much. To see him. To work with him today. To see him hurt and to understand there was nothing she could do about it. To refuse to remarry and know it was the right decision.

It made something inside her feel a little bit dead. But she'd asked for their dealings to be official from now on, and she had to stick to that.

'Being the King is a very big job,' she told Felix. 'He's trying to do the best he can, and that takes time.'

'Louis says I'll make a great king one day too. He says I can sit on a horse like a champion.'

'Did you enjoy it?'

'It was ace. Pierre came too. He's Hilda's grandson and he likes all the stuff I like. Louis let him ride a big black horse. Today I had to ride a little fat pony called Grizelda but that's only because I'm not very good yet. And because they're worried I might fall off onto my leg. But I want to ride one of the big ones.'

'You do what Louis tells you,' she said, startled.

'Yeah, but Pierre's horse is awesome. Mum, when *will* we get to see Papa? I thought he might have time to read to me tonight.'

'He'll come when he has time.'

He glowered. 'Like he didn't come to Australia for nine years?'

'Felix, that was my fault. I knew he was busy so I told him we didn't need him.'

'So tell him we need him now.'

'Do we need him?'

'Yes,' Felix said sleepily. 'He's my papa.'

'He's the King.'

'He should be able to be both,' Felix said fretfully.

'He's doing important stuff.'

'What's more important than us?' Felix demanded, but then sleep began to get the better of him and a difficult conversation was closed.

He slept.

Ellie returned to her own apartment. There was a state dinner happening downstairs. Josef had asked her if she wished to attend but she'd looked at him incredulously.

She settled down with a book but the pages blurred before her.

What's more important than us?

It was a line she could have used years ago, she thought. Standing in the airport, waving goodbye to her husband.

What's more important than us?

Everything.

* * *

The dinner was vital, ponderous, boring. Because he'd spent so much of today at the hospital, the royal boxes were waiting for him as soon as his guests left but, by the look of his guests, that wouldn't happen any time soon.

His ministers were here, a group appointed by his uncle. Marc was the youngest man in the room and the conversation after the third or fourth drink was stultifying.

He'd sent Josef to invite Ellie—as mother of the future King, his ministers had wished to meet her—but he was pleased she hadn't come. She would have been bored witless.

Except he wanted her to be here. She would have met these pompous dignitaries and maybe she'd have dared a smile at him. Ponderous men in black suits, with portly abdomens and ruddy complexions. Overweight matrons, dripping jewels, full of their own importance. Heart attacks waiting to happen. Strokes. They could have bet on who did and didn't have type two diabetes.

Practically all of them?

The gentleman beside him was indulging in a tirade about money being needed for a new race track. It seemed the track was no longer suitable for international events, and the members' room was a disgrace!

Ellie would have seen the ridiculous side of this night.

But she didn't want any part of it, and he didn't blame her.

He glanced at his watch. Eleven-thirty.

Even if they left now it was too late to go to her, even if she hadn't stipulated their contact from now on should be only official. Besides, he had today's boxes and tomorrow's boxes and tomorrow's Very Important Meetings to think about, plus all the meetings he'd missed today.

He looked again at the self-important dignitaries around his table and he knew the meetings were important. This country needed sweeping changes. Race courses were not a priority, but there were so many priorities they were doing his head in.

Ellie had suggested he share the burden, but how could he do that? Who could he trust?

No one, he thought grimly, looking at each of his ministers in turn. Each of these men had been lining their own pockets for years.

His thoughts went back to Ellie and stayed there.

He'd trust her with his life but that was a joke.

She didn't want his life, and why should she?

'Gentlemen, a toast to our new King.' One of the men was on his feet, wavering a little on legs that were distinctly unsteady. 'May he continue to keep this country as comfortable as it's always been.'

In your dreams, Marc thought, eyeing the minister with dislike.

There was, though, a tiny voice in the back of his mind saying, *What if?* What if he let things go on as they were? What if he let these people do what they pleased, as they'd done for years? Maybe then he could have time for medicine.

And time for Ellie.

He knew he couldn't. There was no one he could trust but himself, and he had to face it.

Upstairs, Ellie and Felix were sleeping. As soon as the coronation was done they'd return to Australia and he'd be alone.

So what was new?

Oh, for heaven's sake. He was getting maudlin, and he hadn't even touched the port.

To hell with this. He rose, ostensibly to answer the toast.

'Thank you, and thank you for attending tonight,' he told them. 'Stay on as long as you wish but I'm afraid I have pressing matters needing my attention.'

He turned and left. When he reached the foot of the grand staircase he hesitated.

Upstairs was Ellie.
Official contact only.
The boxes were waiting.
Duty won.

The days turned into weeks faster than Ellie could imagine.

It was a holiday with a difference. Leisure didn't suit her. Being busy did.

She woke early each morning, pulled on her running shoes and headed off around the castle wall before Felix woke. It was a decent half hour hike, making her satisfactorily puffed, satisfactorily tired, and it helped her sleep at night. She and Felix then had breakfast together. Marc was well into his day's meetings by the time they ate, but she wouldn't think of that.

After breakfast Felix headed off with Pierre to listen to whatever tutor had been allocated to the boys that day. Ellie went to the hospital. Under guard. She was deemed part of the royal family and therefore someone requiring protection.

In the emergency ward, though, she could forget about being royal. The staff there seemed to forget too. They were simply too busy to notice. Every time she turned around there was another patient to see. That was the way she liked it, although the obvious need was troubling.

'His Royal Highness promised more staff,' the young doctor she'd worked with on the first day told her. 'But it'll take years. The university courses have been starved of funds. What doctors we do have soon leave because the pay and conditions are so bad. But now, with Prince Marc… he gives the country a sense of hope.'

'It might be useful if he could spend a few hours a day hands-on,' Ellie retorted, but the young doctor shook his head.

'It wouldn't be seemly. He did it once. We can't ask him to do it again.'

Felix saw him in the evenings—they both did. Often he had dinners, meetings, interminable work, but after that first night he'd made a new rule.

'The hours between five and seven are mine to spend with my son,' he'd told Josef, and he had ignored all of Josef's protests.

And Ellie was included, for those two precious hours. She should back off, she thought. This was the time for Marc to form a long-term relationship with his son and that relationship had to be separate from her.

So she shouldn't stick around as Marc listened with every sign of enjoyment to everything Felix had done that day.

'I'm doing so well on the pony that I'm sure I could ride that ginormous black stallion you ride. But Louis says it's a mount fit for a king, and I'll be a king some day, but not yet...'

Then there was, 'I know all our borders now, and who'll be at the coronation, and who I have to meet, and Pierre helps, and sometimes it's interesting...'

And all about his regime of exercise to get strength back in his leg. 'I hate using crutches. I'm sure I could manage without...'

To all this Marc listened with interest and sympathy and wry smiles. And then they'd head down to the palace lawns and maybe swim in the massive solar-heated pool—or watch Felix swim. And if Marc just happened to tug himself out of the pool and sit beside Ellie while Felix kept swimming it seemed entirely natural. It could even fit with her decree of *official only*. They were supervising while their kid messed around in the water.

Marc asked about her day and she tried not to see the hunger in his eyes as he listened to her account of what had happened in the ER.

Then he told her about his day, a clipped version that she knew was edited to make it seem manageable. And Ellie listened and tried not to care. She tried not to feel as if she was getting to know the man rather than the boy she'd married. She tried not to feel the sweet siren call of those moments where she could almost pretend they were family.

She tried not to fall deeper and deeper in love…

Finally Josef would come to find him and Felix and Ellie were left to entertain themselves for the evening.

'Why can't you stay longer with us?' Felix demanded the week before the coronation was due to take place, and Marc sighed.

'There's too much to do, Felix.'

'So what are you doing tonight?'

'I'm entertaining three royal princes from over the border for dinner and then I'm helping Josef plan the seating for the state banquet before the coronation. Only the most important people are invited and, believe it or not, important people are fussy about who they get to sit beside.'

'That's silly. Make them come out and have hamburgers by the pool.'

'I wish.' His smile was rueful. 'Believe it or not, important people often like fuss.'

'Well, I don't,' Felix said fretfully. 'Just stick everyone's names in a hat and pull them out.

'Tempting, but it might cause problems.'

'Will you sit beside Mum?'

Marc glanced at her, raising a quizzical eyebrow.

'I've asked your mother. She won't come.'

'Isn't she important enough?' Felix demanded.

'She's the most important of all, but I can't make her.'

'It's not suitable,' Ellie managed, trying—and failing—to drag her gaze from Marc's. *Please don't look at me like this*, she thought desperately. *Please…*

'But you're going to the coronation,' Felix demanded, suddenly anxious. 'I'm not going by myself.'

'I'll come to the coronation,' Ellie muttered and then thought that sounded incredibly ungracious. 'I mean, it's a generous invitation and of course I accept.' She plucked a blade of grass, though the way these gardens were manicured, each blade was probably numbered for security reasons.

Years ago that was a thought she might have shared with Marc and made him laugh. But not now.

She wasn't game to make him laugh now. She wasn't game to get any closer.

'The coronation can't take place without you,' Marc was telling Felix, with a last look at Ellie before focusing again on his son. 'You both need to be there.'

'And I have to ride the fat old horse.' He looked mutinous. 'Louis says.'

'Felix, you'll be in the royal procession. A fat old horse is better than no horse.'

'But I want to ride a big black one like yours. And I want Mum to ride one too.'

'I'll be sitting in the cathedral, keeping your seat warm.' Ellie told him. 'Felix, we've gone through this. You're royal but I'm not. I stay in the background.'

'And we have to go home straight after the coronation?' Felix still looked mutinous.

'We must. We live in Australia.'

'What if I want to live here? With Papa?'

Ellie sighed, suddenly so tired she couldn't find the energy to answer. She rose and tucked a towel around her bathing suit. This place was unreal, she thought, this garden, this swimming pool, this palace, this...man.

This was Marc's world. Her world was Borrawong. *Never the twain shall meet*, she thought, but right now Borrawong seemed very far away.

And here came Josef again, to remind Marc that his life was waiting inside the palace. The life they couldn't share.

'There's always a place for you here,' Marc said. He was speaking to Felix but she knew the words were intended for her too. 'Any time you want to come... We'll pay for locums, as we're paying now. Any time you need time out from Borrawong...'

'Why would we need time out from Borrawong?' she demanded. 'That's where our life is. Felix, when you're an adult you can decide where you want to live but, for the time being, your home is with me. Felix, let's just enjoy the next few days. We'll watch your papa be crowned King and then we'll go home.'

He came at midnight. The faint tap on her door was of someone unsure if she was asleep or not, so she still had the choice.

Except somehow she knew he'd sense she was awake. Somehow she knew he needed to talk, that this wasn't a social call.

And somehow she knew she didn't have a choice.

She was wearing her faded nightgown, pink with grey and white spots. She'd scrubbed her face. Her curls were tangling every which way around her face.

She'd gone to bed at ten but failed to sleep and that was what she looked like, but calling out to wait until she was respectable wasn't going to work.

Besides, Marc was... Marc had been her husband. He'd seen her in a nightgown before.

He'd seen her in a lot less.

And that was enough of thinking like that, she told herself as she stumped across the room. She'd do annoyance, she told herself. She'd tell him to go away. Make an official appointment. Anything that had to be said should be said in the far safer light of day.

On that thought, she hauled open the door. And blinked. Marc.

No. This wasn't Marc. This was His Royal Highness, the Crown Prince of Falkenstein.

The dinner he'd just attended had been a royal occasion. It would have been disrespectful of him to attend wearing anything less than monarchical splendour. His dark suit. The slashes of gold. The royal insignia. Even his face seemed darker, more regal.

The new King of Falkenstein.

It was all she could do not to slam the door and whimper.

But he was already inside, setting her gently aside so he could close the door behind him.

'I don't…I don't…'

'It's okay,' he told her, hauling off his beautiful jacket and tossing it casually on the back of a chair. As if it wasn't worth a month's salary or more. 'I'm not here to claim husbandly privileges. But we need to talk. Ellie, please stop looking at me like that.'

'I feel like Cinders in her kitchen when the Prince came calling,' she muttered. 'And don't tell me they lived happily ever after because I don't believe it. Sure, he'd have carted her off to his castle but then he'd have headed off to his gold boxes or his royal meetings or his whatever it is all you kings do and she'd be left feeling stupid, sitting around all day in her glass slippers.'

'I've already said if you stay we could organise you to work in the hospital.'

'Why would I stay?'

'Because we loved one another once. Because the pull's getting stronger and we need to give us more time. You must feel it too.'

'Is that what you came to say? Then don't. If the pull's getting stronger, all the more reason for me to leave.'

'Ellie, what's between us…'

'Needs to be forgotten.' She wanted to be a pink puddle, oozing downward in her spots, disappearing between the ancient floorboards. But what was between them had to be faced.

He was watching her with those eyes she'd fallen in love with. With eyes that had seen into her heart—and maybe still did. It was so hard to say it, but she thought this was an honourable man. He deserved the truth.

'That night in the kitchen…' she managed. 'We kissed. And I knew…' At the look on his face she held her hands up, defensive. 'But, regardless of how we feel, it means nothing. Or nothing for the future.'

She looked down, focusing weirdly on Marc's hands. They were good hands, she thought inconsequentially. Surgeon's hands.

'Ellie, all I ask for is another few weeks,' he said. 'You don't need to make a decision about our future now, but you could work here for a while, think about us.'

'How would that make it better?' Her voice sounded as if it came from a long way away but she couldn't help it. It was as if part of her was dissociated from herself.

The Ellie of ten years ago would have reached up, taken his darling face in her hands and kissed that beautiful mouth. She would have melted into his body. She would have surrendered.

But this wasn't the Ellie of ten years ago. This was an Ellie who'd lived with choices, who'd seen the heartbreak that surrendering could cause.

Marc had walked away. He'd had no choice, as she'd had no choice, but the pain…

And that other choice that had lain before her—to give up her baby. If she'd gone down that road…

She shuddered. 'I loved you once,' she whispered, trying to sort it in her own mind. 'And it's true, I love you still. But Marc, I gave you up for your country and that allegiance still holds. If Felix and I stayed here we'd fit in around the edges, wouldn't we? You're giving up your medicine, which is part of you. You're giving it up for noble reasons, but it's still a part of you that's being ripped out. Felix and I can't be yet another part that can be ripped out whenever it's required. You can't ask that of us.'

'I'm not.'

'You are,' she said steadily. 'And yes, maybe it'd be a noble calling, to be your wife again.' She paused and blinked as the repercussions of that path crashed home. 'For heaven's sake, I'd be the Queen.' And that was enough to make her even more sure. 'Marc, no amount of time could make me accept that role. To stay here and take whatever slivers of time you have left, to know that Felix and I always come second, it would break something in me that was shattered ten years ago and has still only partly healed. Let me go home, Marc, to the medicine I love, to the people who need me.'

'I need you.'

'You don't.' Then she shook her head. 'No, that's unfair. It's that you can't need me. You know you can't let yourself need me or need Felix because your country needs you more. We tried once, Marc, and we failed. Let's leave it at that.'

So that was that. No arguments. Nothing. He knew she was right. She could see it in the blank stoicism on his face.

How much did this hurt? How much would it always hurt?

His body was ramrod-stiff. He was holding himself as a soldier, but she saw loss, longing—love? All the things that made her want to reach for him, hold him, cradle him against her. He was a prince, a soldier, a surgeon, but he was so much more.

It took all the will in the world not to reach out and hug him. To agree to whatever he wanted.

'Attend the ball with me,' Marc said, suddenly urgent, and she flashed a scared look at him.

'Why?'

'Because it's the only time.' He took a deep breath. 'That's what I came here to ask. Ellie, everything you're saying is true, but do this one last thing for me. The palace will put pressure on me to marry again and that's unthinkable. I already feel married. In your short time here, you've made an impression on the people. Your work at the hospital has been reported in the media. You'll be going home to Australia to continue with your medicine and the media will respect that. They'll see that you're doing your duty. But, for this last time, we're separating because we have no choice and I'd like to make that a public statement. Come with me, dance with me, be my wife one last time.'

'I can't…' she said weakly and then, even more weakly, 'I don't have a thing to wear.'

And his weary face creased into a smile. It was a resigned smile and, though it didn't light his eyes, it was a smile just the same.

'We can fix that,' he told her. 'Come to the ball and be a princess. Being royal is something I need to live with for the rest of my life but, for one night, Ellie, share my crown.'

'For one night.'

'Yes,' he said steadily. 'And then you can watch the coronation and go home.'

'Marc…'

'This one thing, Ellie. It's all I'm asking.'

And what was a woman to say to that? How could she deny him?

'One night,' she told him. 'Like Cinderella, until midnight. But that's it. Royal's what you are, not me. I'll see you crowned and then I'm going home.'

His valet was waiting for him. Marc had never in his life thought he'd have any use for a valet. In truth, the day he'd moved into the palace he'd told Josef that Ernst should be retired.

Ernst had served his grandfather and his uncle. He was creaky with age. He could no longer manage to pull on the hessian boots Marc's grandfather had worn and Marc now needed to wear for ceremonial occasions. Indeed, there was little he could do.

But on that first night, when the dignitaries had assembled for that interminable dinner, Ernst had adjusted the insignia on Marc's chest, tweaked his clothes until he was up to snuff—and then gone through all the names Marc would meet that night. He'd started tentatively but, once encouraged, he'd spelt out, simply but with brutal frankness, a character assessment of each and what Marc should look out for.

And Marc knew the unspoken truth that such a service hadn't been provided for his uncle or his grandfather. That Ernst, as well as most of the kingdom, was imbued with a sense of hope.

So Ernst stayed, his stooped yet dignified figure waiting now to assist Marc to remove his uniform and take it away to places unseen to polish and clean and press.

Marc was accustomed to the old man's presence now; in fact he almost found it a comfort. Ernst seemed to know when to speak and when not to speak.

Tonight he looked at Marc's face and stayed silent. He gathered Marc's uniform, gave a small formal bow and would have left. Marc stopped him.

'Ernst?'

'Yes, sir?'

'Could you tell—? Hell, I don't know *who* you tell, but could you tell someone that Dr Carson will be requiring a ball gown?'

The old man's face lit up. 'We can have a dressmaker here first thing in the morning—or after Dr Carson gets back from the hospital. This is good news, sir.'

'She's only staying until the coronation. I'd like her to stay afterwards, but it's impossible.'

'Yes, sir.' Ernst's face was once again inscrutable. He paused as if considering. 'If I could ask, sir…why?'

'She's a doctor. She has her own life.' And then he thought, *Why not say it like it is?* 'I had to leave her ten years ago because of the war,' he confessed. 'How can I promise never to leave her again? There are demands on my time everywhere.'

Ernst hesitated. 'Your uncle, your grandfather, they never allowed their royal duties to interfere with what they thought was important.'

'And look where that got the country.'

'Yes, sir,' Ernst said softly, and he opened the door and turned to leave. 'But you, sir, will be a very different monarch to those who came before you. It will be up to you to decide what's important, and what isn't.'

He left. Marc headed to the great canopied affair that served as the royal bed. He lay and stared up at the ornate room, lit by the moonlight still flooding in the windows.

This bed was huge. *Dumb.*

He was destined to sleep in it for ever.

And Ellie? She was sleeping in a bed just as big, but hers was temporary. In the morning she'd have breakfast with Felix and then head to the hospital.

He'd have meeting after interminable meeting, all of which were important.

He thought of Ernst's words. *It will be up to you to decide what's important.*

Ha.

Ellie knew what was important, he thought. She'd made the decision to raise Felix herself. She'd fought to make it through medicine, to do the work she loved.

Lucky Ellie.

Desirable Ellie. Beautiful Ellie. Ellie, the woman he wanted to hold, *for as long as we both shall live.*

They'd made that vow.

So keep it!

And drag Ellie into this goldfish bowl? Assure her there'd be no more crises? Assure her his country would always come second after his marriage?

He swore, threw back the covers and headed for the window. Here he could see the distant moonlit mountains. His country. Full of his people. People he'd helped until now with his hands, with his medicine, but people he needed to help now with so much more.

He ached to be at the hospital. His fingers ached to be doing the job he was trained for.

And along the vast palace hall was Ellie. And his son. His family. He ached to be there too.

To have and to hold. That was what he'd promised. But to hold in this place, knowing there were no guarantees? That life could rip them apart again?

How could he ask Ellie to share a life he loathed?

CHAPTER TEN

THE PROBLEM WITH coronations was that they involved parties. Not just for the royal family and those in close proximity, but for the entire country.

And with parties came trouble.

Some of the hardest times in a hospital emergency department were Christmas afternoon, with its gut traumas from overeating and its appalling injuries from trying out new 'toys', and New Year's Eve when it seemed the whole world set out to get drunk.

The coronation of the King of Falkenstein was like a combination of both these events—only bigger.

Two days had been deemed public holidays—the day before the coronation and the day of the coronation itself. The theory was that the country could party hard the day before, then watch the coronation, take a wee nap and get on with life.

The day before the coronation Ellie headed to the hospital as usual. She had the ball that night, but it had her so nervous she was glad she had work to block it out.

Felix was busy—he was having a last practice on his horse with Pierre. 'You should see my uniform,' he breathed to Ellie at breakfast. 'They've even made the trouser leg wider so it can hide my brace. If only I had a bigger horse, I'd look bee*yoo*tiful.'

'You'll look beautiful anyway,' Ellie told him as she

left. She watched with a mixture of pride and worry as he scooted off with Pierre to learn to be a prince.

The hospital was the only place where worry could take a back seat to need.

The morning was quiet but the workload soon built. She usually finished by two, but by then there was already a rush. A warm summer's day, too much alcohol, too many kids doing stupid things...

A teenager arrived with a slashed arm from a broken beer bottle just as she was about to go off duty. He was drunk and belligerent and there was no one else to control him.

She sent a message to Hilda and Felix and set about quieting the kid down so she could stitch him.

And tried not to think of Marc.

What would he be doing now? Practising his dance steps? Polishing his speech?

'There's no need to be bitter,' she told herself, and somehow she'd said it out loud.

'I'm not bitter,' the kid she was treating declared. 'I'm pissed.'

'And lucky,' she retorted. 'A fraction to the left and you'd have sliced a vein.'

'I'd have bled for my King and country,' the kid boasted.

Yeah, right.

And then, of course, the appalling happened, as it did so often in the emergency departments of hospitals around the world. A family party. Accelerant used to boost the barbecue. The container left open and too close to the fire. The inevitable.

Eight children and fifteen adults with burns from the flash explosion.

The hospital was running on a skeleton staff anyway—something about extra pay rates for the public holiday. An emergency call went out for doctors to come in. Two responded, which meant they were staffed with four doctors, including Ellie.

Major burns.

'Maybe we could ring M… His Highness,' she said tentatively as she realised the enormity of the need, but the director wouldn't hear of it.

'Disturb His Majesty on this of all days? He's at parliament right now, taking the official oaths. Tomorrow is the crowning but today is just as important. To drag him away…his priority must be his country.'

'At least let him decide,' Ellie muttered but the director shook his head.

'His Majesty is no longer a doctor. He's our King and all the people here would agree that he's needed as our leader.'

And so he was, Ellie thought. She was splitting her time between two patients, a girl of three and a boy of six. The blast had been low and spread upward. The kids had been playing close so they both had vicious burns to their legs. The rest of their bodies were blessedly unmarked but it'd take all her skill and more to prevent amputation.

She had both kids in an induced coma and that worried her too. She needed a specialist anaesthetist.

She wanted Marc. She wanted his skill, but she also realised that she wanted his authority—to call in specialists, to kick butt to get things done.

He was being sworn in by parliament so that long-term he could fix this mess, she told herself.

And as she worked on through the long afternoon and evening something settled inside her. This was an emergency and yes, it would be great if he was here, hands-on, but how many emergencies were being played out around the country right now? How many hospitals were understaffed? How many children like the little girl whose leg she was dressing needed skilled doctors? The only way they could be provided was if someone—Marc—accepted that he couldn't be here now.

But *she* was here. She worked on, oblivious to outside needs. Hilda would be caring for Felix. He had Pierre, he was used to medical imperatives, he'd be okay.

And Marc? She'd promised to attend the ball, but if Marc didn't understand medical need no one would.

At nine at night Ellie finally emerged from the wards to speak to the relatives of the kids she'd been working on. Aunts, uncles, grandparents were all burdened with unspeakable anxiety.

'She should be okay,' Ellie told the little girl's family. 'It'll be a long road to recovery but we've relieved the pressure. There'll be scarring, she'll need specialist attention, but we're confident she'll recover. Her parents are sleeping in chairs by her bed, so maybe you could go home and do the same? The family will need you in the long road ahead.'

'We won't go home,' the grandmother told her. 'This is our son, our daughter, our granddaughter. This is where our hearts are. This is where we stay.'

'You're tired…'

'We can be tired when we're no longer needed. Thank you, Doctor,' the woman said simply. 'You go and rest. It's you who must be tired.'

She was tired but she'd been this tired before. She talked to the little boy's family, then walked out through the throng of gathered relatives and thought that two children were alive, their scars hopefully minimised, because of her presence today. She thought, *it felt okay.*

She thought of Marc, who'd spent his day in ceremonial clothing, ticking off box after box of his long list of coronation duties, and she thought he'd be so much more tired than she was.

This is where our hearts are.

The grandmother's words came back to her, and her heart twisted.

Her bodyguards were waiting. A chauffeur was holding a car door wide.

She slipped into the luxurious interior and closed her eyes.

The ball would have started.

All she wanted was to hug Felix and then sleep. But, tucked away at the back of her heart, was another desire. To go to Marc as she'd done for those few short months all those years ago. To be held by him, comforted by him, find solace and joy in his body. In his love.

Yeah, that's not going to happen, she thought bleakly, but she thought again of Marc and what he'd faced today.

This is where our hearts are.

When the car pulled up at the palace, Hilda met her and gave her a hug and she took it gratefully.

'We hear you've done amazing work,' Hilda said simply. 'Our people are grateful. His Highness knows what you've been doing—he was briefed a couple of hours ago. He expresses his gratitude and says if you don't wish to attend the ball he understands. Felix is asleep. I can run you a bath, give you some supper and you can sleep.'

And that was a siren song. A bath, supper and then sleep.

But those words kept echoing.

This is where our hearts are.

We can be tired when we're no longer needed.

Did Marc need her? He didn't, she thought. He couldn't. They'd made that mutual decision years ago.

But for now...

For now, even though her day had been tough, she knew without being told that Marc's had been worse, trapped in bureaucracy, in ceremonial imperatives.

We can be tired when we're no longer needed.

He couldn't need her for ever. She was going home, but for now, for tonight, maybe her presence might help. It was an indulgent thought, probably stupid, but he'd wanted her to attend the ball. It had seemed important.

He'd organised her a gown.

So, as doctors did the world over, she fought for and found a second wind. She braced and smiled at Hilda and moved onto the next thing.

'A bath would put me to sleep,' she told her. 'A shower and a sandwich—and then my ball gown, please. I have a Cinderella moment I need to attend to.'

Ten o'clock and already the night had been interminable.

He'd spent an hour every afternoon for almost two weeks with a dancing master. It had chafed him to absolute fury, but Josef had deemed it imperative.

'The dances at ceremonial balls are set pieces. Every Royal in Europe is trained from birth. Not to dance would be deemed an insult, to dance badly a bigger one.'

So politics demanded he danced. Politics demanded he looked like something out of the archaic portraits lining his ancestral hall.

Politics demanded he danced with one 'imperative' after another while he knew Ellie was coping with far more important things. Like saving lives.

Except this was important. Cooperation with neighbouring countries was crucial to stability. He needed to gain the trust of the dignitaries here tonight and one of the ways to do that was to show he respected their world.

Thus he danced when all he wanted was to be with Ellie.

He'd sent word to find out how things were panning out. 'The crisis is over,' Josef had told him half an hour ago. 'The specialists you had flown in have arrived. There are now enough medical staff on the ground to handle the work and we seem to have got off without fatalities.' He'd given a small smile, which was huge for Josef. 'If we're not careful we'll have your Ellie acclaimed as a national heroine. She stands to be as popular as you are.'

'Except she's going home.'

Josef's smile had died. 'As you say.'

'She won't come now.'

Josef had glanced at his watch and agreed. 'Our people tell me she's been overwhelmed by work from this morning. I believe we must excuse her. At least there's no imperative. For your wife not to attend would be an insult but at least she's not your wife.'

And how lucky was that? Marc thought grimly, and went to do his duty.

He danced. He felt ill about Ellie.

And then, as he danced with the Queen Mother of a neighbouring country, there was a stir at the door and he glanced across. It was Ellie.

She looked absurdly nervous. Absurdly self-conscious.

She looked stunning.

Who had designed her gown? Maybe Ellie had decreed its style herself, he thought, for in this ballroom full of glitz and tizz, of diamonds and gold, of chandeliers, of pure unmitigated opulence, Ellie stood apart.

Wearing anything but a beautiful ball gown in this magnificent place would have been yet another of those thousand chasms that could be construed as a royal insult. But this was built with elegance as well as simplicity. It had a scooped sweetheart neckline, tiny sleeves, a figure-hugging bodice and a skirt that flared in soft folds, sweeping all the way to the floor.

The gown had no embellishments. Its beauty was in the cloth itself, Marc thought, shot silk or some such. It was sapphire showered with the merest shadows of silver, making it shimmer as she moved.

She'd caught her hair in a simple knot so her auburn curls were escaping. Simple and yet beautiful.

She was wearing a single pearl at her throat, and his own throat seemed to constrict as he realised it was the pearl he'd given her for the only one of her birthdays they'd been together.

She looked stunning. Ethereal. Breathtaking. But she was standing in the doorway looking scared to death.

Marc turned to the woman he'd been dancing with. 'Will you excuse me, madam? I need to go to my wife.'

'Your ex-wife, surely?' But there was a smile playing at the corners of the Queen Mother's lips.

'Is there such a thing?' Marc murmured. 'For me, I'm not sure.' And he bowed and turned and strode through the dancers to Ellie. The couples parted before him. He reached Ellie and he couldn't think of a thing to say.

'Hey.' How inane was that?

'Hey, yourself.' She looked at him with relief. 'Thank you for coming to rescue me.'

'Thank you for coming.' He smiled down at her, thinking she was more beautiful than anyone in the room. Her face was pale and her eyes were too large in her face. She wore minimal make-up—she must have dressed in a hurry—and he recognised her shadows. She'd spent too long in the emergency room, fighting to save lives. But, oh, she was lovely.

'My people tell me you've done some stunning work,' he told her, his eyes not leaving hers.

'We were lucky. No fatalities. But, Marc, there might have been. More doctors…'

'There will be more doctors,' he swore. 'I appointed a new Minister for Health yesterday, an excellent woman. She knows what you've been doing and she intends to personally thank you before you leave. But, Ellie…' he held out his hand '…for tonight can we forget about today and forget about tomorrow? For now… I seem to remember you can dance.'

He thought of that first time they'd gone out for a pub dinner all those years ago. A pianist had started up— honky-tonk, jazz, fun. And Ellie had laughed with delight and grabbed his hand and dragged him out to the dance floor. 'Let's jive.'

'This isn't the music I'm used to,' she muttered now. There was a thirty-piece orchestra centre stage, playing a classical waltz.

'So you're not up to it?' His eyes gleamed a challenge and the ready laughter sprang back into hers.

'Are you kidding? Bring it on.'

Forget the jive. The waltz was much better.

She hadn't waltzed, not properly, since she was eight years old and her grandma died. But that memory was deeply embedded. Ellie's mother had been ill, flighty, reckless. There'd been many nights when her mother had simply disappeared. But she remembered her grandmother being there, turning up their sound system, putting on the songs she'd learned to dance to.

Dancing with her Grandma, Ellie had felt special, safe, loved.

That was how she felt now—only so much more.

Safe? That was a weird description, she thought. The eyes of everyone in the ballroom were on them. She was a country bumpkin, child of a single mum, a kid from the wrong side of the tracks. Watching her, society's elite. She should be nervous, self-conscious, achingly aware of all the things she could do wrong.

But the day had blown away any last vestige of self-consciousness. She'd fought all day for the things that really mattered.

And here, right now, for this moment, was the only thing that mattered. Marc was holding her in his arms. Her steps were magically following his. His eyes were smiling at her, the music was all around them and the rest of the world faded to nothing.

'You do know how much I love you?' His words were a soft murmur, a background to the amazing music, maybe part of the music itself. 'What you've done today... I'm so proud of you, Ellie.'

'Don't,' she begged. 'I can't stay.'

'I'm not asking you to.' He swung her around, his arm encircling her waist. The silky folds of her skirt brushed her legs. *We might just as well be making love*, she thought, in the tiny part of her brain that was still available for thought. 'Ellie, it was unfair of me to ask. But we have tonight. It ended at midnight for the Prince too, remember?'

'Cinderella, huh?'

'I'm thinking they were both blasted out of their worlds. In fairy tales they get to fudge the ending—happy ever after. But in real life...'

'In real life the Prince has to get up the morning after, put on a suit and tie and discuss the state of the country's... I don't know...sewer system.'

His lips twitched. 'We do have to discuss that.'

'There you go, then. Where's the romance?'

'Here, tonight.' The turn of the dance brought them close again, and his lips brushed her hair. She could hear a collective gasp from around them.

'Marc, don't. They'll get the wrong impression.'

'No,' he said strongly and swung her again. 'They'll get the right impression. Josef talks of me finding a wife. I did find one. She's free to return to her own life and I understand the reasons she's going, but there's no need for me to find anyone else. Ever.'

She didn't last until midnight. Cinderella's Prince might have danced with his Cinders to the exclusion of everyone else, but this was no fairy tale, and after a full set in Marc's arms Josef was casting them anxious looks. Royal noses were being put out of joint. They both knew it, but it was Ellie who tugged herself out of Marc's arms and forced herself to break the moment.

'You know you should be dancing with someone else.'

'Someones else,' he said ruefully. 'Josef's given me a list.'

'And I'm asleep on my feet.' Though it hadn't been true until now. It was only now Marc had released her that she felt like sagging.

'I wish…'

'We both wish.' She managed to smile. 'I should have excused myself tonight.'

'I'm glad you didn't.'

'It felt…important. To come.'

'It was.'

Josef was looking directly at Marc. Marc was ignoring him but Ellie saw the look. It contained a hint of desperation.

'I won't say good luck tomorrow,' she whispered, speaking fast, knowing this was the last time they'd speak in anywhere approaching privacy. 'You won't need it. You'll be a brilliant king.'

'Thank you for bringing Felix.'

'He's told me all about tomorrow. He's going to look as "beeyootiful" as you, apart from riding on a fat horse.'

'She's not fat.' Marc gave her a lopsided smile that said he was under as much pressure as she was. 'When Felix comes back next year without the brace he can have quite a different mount, but for a kid with no riding experience, with his leg in a brace, in a royal procession…'

'Hey, you don't need to convince me. I'm his mother.'

'And I'm his father. I wish I could…'

'Don't wish.' She took his hands. She would have raised her face and kissed him—every ounce of her wanted to—but in this place, under the eye of the world's media and royalty…maybe not. 'Just be,' she told him. 'I'll be watching you from my place in the cathedral. Josef's arranged for Felix to be escorted to join me after the procession. We'll both be cheering for you like crazy.'

'And then going back to Australia.'

'Yes,' she said and smiled at Josef, a wide, encompassing smile that said she was done, Josef could do his worst. 'Yes,' she said again and pressed his hands hard, just the once, and then released them. 'Goodnight, Your Highness, and goodbye. Tomorrow you'll be too busy to see me, and the day after that I'll be gone.'

And she turned away, made sure her smile stayed pinned to her face, and walked away.

Through the glittering throng. Out the magnificent entrance. Down the steps to the waiting car.

And I have nothing to leave behind, she thought, and even managed a feeble smile. *Not even a glass slipper.*

CHAPTER ELEVEN

ELLIE SLEPT BADLY—okay, she hardly slept at all—but some time before dawn she fell into an uneasy doze. Her dreams were troubled, a jumble of royal impressions—the ball, the palace—plus the day she'd had treating burned kids. And interspersed amongst it all was Marc. Marc, looking at her with troubled eyes, hungry eyes. Marc, who would have held her, but who understood too well why she couldn't stay.

Marc was just down the hall. He was as far from her now as he'd always been. But, strangely, she seemed to know him better now. She knew the man he was—the honour and duty that would hold him to his lonely course.

It broke her heart, but to follow his suggestion, to remarry... To let herself fall again...

Except hadn't she already? Would she once again break her heart as they parted?

When a knock at her door finally roused her, for a wild, half-asleep moment she thought, she hoped, it might be him. She glanced at the bedside clock and it was after eight.

Yikes. She sat up with a start, practicalities overtaking dreams. Felix had to be in his uniform and ready by nine. Hopefully, Hilda had woken him and given him breakfast.

And the knock couldn't be Marc. She could only imagine the list of formalities he'd be required to complete this morning.

'Yes?' she called.

It was Hilda, opening the door a crack to call through without intruding, 'Good morning, madam.' Her tone was apologetic. 'We let you sleep as long as we could but Felix is needed. Felix, your father's valet wishes to see you dressed...'

What? Ellie sat bolt upright in bed. Hilda thought Felix was here? 'Hilda?'

Hilda's head appeared around the door. 'Madam?'

'Felix isn't here.'

The door opened wider. Hilda stood, plump and perplexed, staring at Ellie's bed as if it were trying to play tricks on her. 'He always comes into bed with you in the mornings.'

'I couldn't sleep,' Ellie stammered. 'I mean, until early. Yesterday, it was so big, and dancing with Marc...' *Oh, for heaven's sake.* She was stammering like an idiot.

'That's why we let you sleep.' Hilda gave a half smile but it didn't last. 'But I checked on Felix an hour ago and his bed was empty. I assumed he was with you.'

'I tucked him in at midnight but he was fast asleep.' She was wide awake now. 'Maybe he's gone to the stables. Or to find Marc? He's very upset that this is our last day.'

'I'll find out,' Hilda said, and disappeared with such alacrity that Ellie realised she had indeed left it until the last moment to find him. And that the normally unflappable lady was close to panic.

She rose and tugged on jeans and a windcheater. The coronation dress made for her by the palace dressmaker, a dress fit for the mother of the future King, hung in state in its own wardrobe but it could wait until later. She headed to Felix's rooms and stared at his rumpled bed.

The bed was cold.

She walked to the window and saw the stables below. Felix loved this room. He'd spent hours sitting on the window ledge watching the stable hands walk the magnificent horses around the exercise yards.

The longing had been there since the first day. 'One day I'll ride a horse like Papa's.'

'When you come back next year you'll have the brace off your leg. Your papa will be able to teach you properly.'

'I don't want to come back. I want to stay now.'

Why did that conversation come back to her now? Why, as she watched Hilda talking to the head groom, why, as she saw men suddenly run, as she saw Hilda turn and look up at her window...?

As she saw fear.

And suddenly she was running too, taking the stairs two at a time, flying down and through the back entrance, heading for Hilda. Who was almost sobbing with fear.

'What...?'

Hilda stopped, couldn't get words out. It was up to the head groom.

'The lad—' he too seemed visibly upset '—he was down early, hanging round, helping the morning feeds. He's often here. He loves this place.'

'I know that.'

'And he's good with the horses,' the man said. 'He was going from stall to stall, feeding them the bits of carrot I always leave on hand because I know he likes feeding them. Usually I'd keep an eye on him but today... There are so many horses to get ready. I guess...' He was struggling, Ellie saw, trying to get his thoughts together. 'I called everyone into the tack room for a few minutes to collect the gear. It was last-minute polish, all hands required to give everything a last buff. And I had to ensure the right tack went on the right horses.'

He was wavering, almost wild-eyed, frantic. 'Just tell me,' Ellie managed.

'So...so we came out and the lad was gone,' he said, catching himself. 'And I thought no more of it until Hilda came running. And then we checked.' And he stopped, as if he couldn't bear to go on.

'And His Majesty's horse is missing,' Hilda whispered. 'The great black stallion Prince Marc is to ride in the ceremonial procession today. It's missing and so is Felix. Oh, ma'am...'

And it was too much for her. Hilda put her hand on her heart and crumpled where she stood.

For a few moments Ellie had to concentrate on Hilda.

Her son was missing. He'd presumably taken Marc's stallion. Her whole body was suffused with panic but Hilda had crumpled and she needed to check it was a simple faint and not a heart attack.

But her pulse was steady. She regained consciousness almost as she hit the ground. She sat up and sobbed and apologised and went into frantic mode again and Ellie released her wrist and called one of the female grooms.

'Can you take Madame Bouchier to her room, please. No, Hilda, there's nothing you can do here. You've had a shock and you need to recover. Have you had breakfast? No? Stay with her,' she told the girl. 'That's an order. Hilda, you lost consciousness and we need to get you checked properly.'

'Felix...' she moaned.

'Is my responsibility.'

And then Josef came hurrying around the corner of the stable yard. Of course. The man was omnipresent in this place; he would have heard of this almost before it happened. He was demanding answers of the security guards, incredulous they didn't have answers. Then moving on.

'Claud,' he snapped. 'Take two of the lads. Ride the horses not in use this morning. Let me know the moment he's found.'

Three men. Ellie turned and gazed up at the great mountain that backed the castle. Three was all they could spare?

But the coronation. The parade. Of course. This was a greater imperative than her son.

She closed her eyes for a millisecond, trying frantically to settle. And when she opened them Marc was there.

He must have been dressing, she thought, though her thoughts were close to hysterics. He was wearing skin-tight breeches. A voluminous white shirt, high-collared but not yet fastened. A crimson and gilt sash. High boots, moulded to his calves, glistening from hours of polish.

'We have things under control, Your Highness,' Josef said, stepping in to stand between Marc and Ellie. As if he knew what a threat such a connection caused.

But the threat was ignored. Marc took the man's shoulders and lifted him aside. His hands caught her waist and he held her, hard and strong.

'What's under control? What's happening?' He glanced around the gathered stable hands, and he got it. 'Where's Felix?'

So Josef had been told, but not Marc.

When Felix was Marc's son...

'We think he's taken your horse,' Ellie managed. 'But, Marc, the coronation...'

'Why would he take my horse?'

His voice was commanding. It was the voice of a king, she thought dazedly, but it was also the voice of a surgeon, a doctor facing drama, a surgeon who needed facts now. It brought her up short. This was how she had to respond.

Triage.

Tell the surgeon the facts.

'He hates riding the mare,' she managed. 'Everything about his feet, everything that's restricted him, he's fought every way he knows how. He knew the mare was chosen because of his leg. And...'

'And?' Marc's gaze was fixed on hers, urgent and compelling. 'And, Ellie?'

She'd only had moments to think what Felix would be

doing but the knowledge had suddenly slammed home. 'You told him, at the start, you said you couldn't be crowned unless he was here. And I told him as soon as the coronation is over we'll go home.' She was struggling to keep her voice level. 'He'll have figured it out his own way. He loves it here.' And how much did it hurt to say it, but there was no way of saying it gently. 'Marc, he loves you.'

She watched his face change. She watched his shoulders sag—and then straighten. Turning to imperatives. 'So he's taken my horse?' He turned to the head groom. 'Is he saddled?'

'No, sir,' the man stammered. 'Just the bridle.'

'Reins?'

'I'll check.'

Ellie almost whimpered. For Felix to balance bareback, with only one leg available to grip... And he could barely ride.

Someone must have heard Felix ride away, Ellie thought numbly, but on this frantic morning hoof beats in the stable yard could well go unmarked. Felix had been lucky.

Or unlucky. The stallion was huge. How had Felix ever managed him?

He was smart. He was brave.

Just like his father.

'He'll have gone up the mountain,' Marc snapped. 'When I rode with him last week I showed him how the gates could be unlocked from the inside. I want every person who can mount a horse up that mountain now. Ring Commander Thierry. He has more mounted men readying for the parade. I want them here too. And saddle Theo for me.'

'Sir!' Josef's was a cry of bewilderment. 'The royal reception starts in thirty minutes. The parade starts in little over an hour. You can't just walk away.'

'I'm not walking away,' Marc said grimly. 'I'm asking them to wait.'

'But for how long?'

'For as long as it takes,' Marc snapped. 'I abandoned my family once for my country. I won't do it again. My country's important but my wife and my son come first.'

She'd been a child when she'd last saddled a horse. She did it now, instinctively, and so fast she was mounted as Marc prepared to lead the first group up the mountain.

His frown intensified as he saw her. 'You don't ride.'

'I chose not to ride. I'm riding now.'

'You'll be needed here. If...when he's found.'

'I'm coming. If anyone else finds him there are radios to let me know.'

He wasted no more time on arguing, just nodded and turned his attention to his horse.

She fell into the tail of the party. The mare she'd saddled was quiet, docile, one of the few not primped for today's ceremony. She seemed to sense Ellie's mood.

She also looked to Marc's horse as if it was the natural leader, and Ellie thought, *You and me both.*

The police commissioner had joined the search on his own mount. His face was as grim as Ellie felt. He fell in beside her and practically glowered. This was her fault?

'You realise we have thousands of people already lining the route. Every detail has been planned for months. For His Highness to disappear...'

'Marc hasn't disappeared,' she retorted. 'He's looking for his son.'

'Yes, but...'

No! She wouldn't listen to him. She wouldn't think about the beautiful uniforms of the searchers, uniforms worn for ceremonial occasions, not for bashing their way up narrow forest trails.

She wouldn't think of Marc, urgent, dark, commanding, seemingly almost one with the horse under him, throwing orders like the commander he was.

And she wouldn't think of Felix.

But that was too big an ask. All she could think of was Felix, small, wiry, braced leg, heading into the wilderness bareback on a stallion he'd never ridden before.

This wasn't a wilderness, she reminded herself, casting for comfort. It was part of the same medieval precinct that encompassed castle and village.

But no one would be up here today. Every soul would be lining the streets or glued to the television to watch the pageantry.

Except the searchers.

How many troops had Marc called in? It must be only half an hour since Felix's absence had been noticed but there were already calls from all over the hillside.

If you lose a child in the forest, do it on a day when half the country seems prepared to mount a horse, Ellie thought, and rode grimly on.

The group divided and divided again as the searchers fanned out, but she stayed behind Marc. Two bodyguards stuck close. Plus the police commissioner. Ellie wanted to talk to Marc but the grim-faced men by his side had her staying back. And what would she say to him anyway?

A man riding beside her gave a surreptitious glance at his watch and winced.

'What?'

'It's half an hour until the procession, ma'am,' he told her apologetically. 'My wife's there, with the kiddies. I'm wondering if they've been told.'

She winced. A whole nation's celebration…

How had she let this happen?

She urged her mare forward and the men around Marc reluctantly gave way to her. The track here was wide enough for two horses. This was the logical way he'd have come, Ellie thought, the widest track leading straight up. But there were cliffs at the side. She couldn't bear to think…

'If he's slipped we'd see the stallion,' Marc said grimly,

hardly acknowledging her presence. 'My horse looks intimidating but he's gentle enough. He knows this mountain and he knows his way home. Dammit, where is he?' The last words were an explosion, a fury so fierce it made the horse he was riding start back. He swore and settled him and Ellie saw the rigid control descend again.

'Marc...'

He cast her a look she'd never seen before. Anguish? Fear? Anger? 'What?'

'I'm so sorry.'

'It needed only that,' he said savagely. 'Don't you dare be sorry. You think this isn't down to me?'

'If I'd agreed to stay...'

'Why would you agree to stay?' He shook his head. 'Ten years ago I made the wrong choice. I was conceited enough to think I'd make a difference.'

'You did make a difference,' she said, struggling to keep her emotion in check. 'I've heard enough of your work during the war. How many people you saved. And afterwards—the health system's flawed, but how much more so would it be if you and your father hadn't fought for it?'

'I can't even keep my son safe.'

'That's my job.' She took a deep breath. 'Marc, stop.' It nearly killed her to say it but it had to be said. 'You have searchers all over the mountain. I know...I know the procession will be smaller without them and I'm not generous enough to send them away, but you, Marc...your country's waiting.'

'You think I can be crowned without my son?' And he cast her another of those looks, with such depth, such despair it almost killed her. 'Without you?'

'Josef would say...'

'Damn what Josef would say,' he muttered. 'Damn what the world will say. A man can be driven only so far. Ten years ago I walked away from you because of imperatives. Those imperatives have only become more urgent, but today, for this day, the imperative of my son, and of you, Ellie, take precedence over all. We'll find him, Ellie,' he said grimly. 'We must. And until then… Until you have your son again, the country can wait.'

And then they found the horse.

They heard a whicker ahead and Marc was off his horse in an instant, holding up his hand for silence. If Felix was ahead, struggling to stay on his mount, the last thing they wanted was to startle him.

They listened and the whicker came again. Close.

Ellie was off her horse too. She didn't think consciously of dismounting. She only knew she had.

'Stay,' Marc told the group around them. 'Silent.' He reached for her hand, imperious, in command. She hardly noticed. She slipped her hand in his and held on tight, and he led her forward.

The track here was steep and treacherously rocky, the climb to the peak rising in earnest. The ground fell sharply on the left, the cliff face too close to the path for comfort.

There were trees, stunted by snowfall, clustered to the right. The bends were sharp and sudden.

'Watch your feet,' Marc told her, but his hand held her, strong and sure, and she knew she couldn't fall. Not while Marc held her.

Oh, but Felix! To try and ride up here…

They edged forward, up and round the bend. And there was Mer Noire, Marc's magnificent stallion. He had his head bent, grazing on a patch of alpine daisies. As he sensed their presence he lifted his magnificent head and whickered again.

He was bareback. No rider.

She had sense enough not to call out, but oh, she almost did. *Felix!* Dear heaven, if he'd been thrown near the drop from the cliffs…

Marc released her hand. He edged forward, speaking

softly to the great horse. Mer Noire let him approach, rearing his head at the last moment and trying to back away, but Marc had him by the bridle and held fast.

'So where's your rider, big boy?' he murmured but he was looking upward. 'Not so far, eh? He'll have been trying to make it to the top.'

'He'll have come off.' She was trying not to sob.

'I imagine so,' Marc said but he said it so matter-of-factly that she found herself illogically reassured. As if coming off was no big deal. 'These bends are tight. Mer Noire doesn't know the meaning of slow or caution and, without a saddle, any stumble could have seen Felix fall. But Mer Noire knows where home is. He wouldn't have kept going up after Felix came off. He'll have been coming down. He'll have stopped because he couldn't resist a snack.'

'But the cliff...'

'The steep drop's behind us. It's only a ten-minute climb to reach the top from here. We'll leave the horses and walk. Come on with me.'

He gave a 'Hoy!' and the rest of the group edged into the clearing. 'We're going up,' Marc told them and received a groan from the police commissioner.

'Sir, the time...'

And Marc told him where he could put his clockwatching. 'Stay here,' he told him. 'Ellie and I will go on alone.'

'But why?' The man was almost sobbing.

'Because he may be on the track, hurt, in which case we'll call you. But it's likely that he's come up here for a purpose and that's to stop my coronation. He knows what pain is and it won't stop him.'

'You think he could be hiding?' Ellie asked, and he put his arm around her and gave her a swift, hard hug.

'That's what I'd have done at his age,' he said dryly. 'And I'm starting to think my son is very like his father.'

So they climbed steadily, hand in hand, towards the peak. It was an extraordinary climb, an extraordinary view out over this beautiful country, but Ellie was in no mood for sightseeing. As they neared the peak she was close to collapse.

'You must be wrong. He must have come off near the cliffs. Oh, Marc...'

But he was looking intently at a branch broken beside the path ahead, at scuff marks and hoof prints in the dust.

'Something's happened here. It has to be a fall, which means he can't be far. He must be hiding.' He tugged his hand free from hers, cupping his hands and started to call.

'Felix, you've done it.' His deep voice echoed out over the mountain, seemingly all the way to the town below. 'You've done what you set out to do. You need to come out now and face us.'

No answer. Marc nodded, as if he expected no less, and started walking further up the track. A hundred yards on he tried again.

No result.

But fifty yards on, third try...

There was a sound very like a sob from the under-growth. 'I...I can't.' A child's voice.

'Oh, Felix!' Ellie had almost given up on breathing she was so afraid, and for a moment she couldn't believe what she'd heard. 'Felix!'

Marc was already on his knees, bashing his way through the bushes. 'Where are you?' His voice was demanding. 'Felix?'

'I can't come out.' Felix's voice was a sob from behind dense undergrowth. 'The coronation hasn't even started yet. I wanted to get to the top and wait but the path was too skinny and the tree hit me in the face. And I fell. And I tried to crawl higher but I can't. And I think I've broken my other leg.'

* * *

What should you do when a child's been so wilfully dis-obedient that he's disrupted an entire nation's plans for a coronation?

You hug him, that's what.

Only Ellie couldn't get near because Marc was before her, gathering him into his arms—carefully, though, so as not to disturb either leg—and holding him tight. Putting his face in Felix's hair. Saying things that Ellie couldn't hear as she fought to get through the undergrowth to join them. Things that silenced Felix's sobs and had him crumpling against his papa.

And then Ellie was with them and she was gathered too. Marc had them both in his arms, holding with a fierceness that was a declaration all by itself. And Ellie was weeping as she hadn't wept for years, giving herself this moment, this one precious sliver of time, to let go of her precious control. To give herself over to the knowledge that Felix was safe and Marc had him in charge, and he had her too, and she was where she was meant to be.

Or not, but that was for the future. For now, there was this one wonderful moment before the world broke in. One moment of stillness.

One moment where her heart knew all the answers, and they were right here with this man.

He kissed Felix, and he kissed her too, lightly, almost a kiss of wonder, but it was enough. It had to be enough.

For then the world broke in, in the form of Marc's body-guards, bashing their way to them, looking frantic—they'd let their liege lord out of their sight and they were suffering. And the police commissioner was behind them. And more searchers were behind them.

And Marc was settling Felix, lying him down again, turning his attention to his legs.

Another broken leg? Reality was sinking back. *How*

bad? After that first glorious moment of exultation Ellie's heart was sinking again. With the bad leg not yet recovered, it'd be back to the wheelchair, back to months of frustration, back to...

'Can you wiggle your toes for me?' Marc asked and Ellie hauled herself away from the other end of the pendulum. Bliss to panic in moments.

'My foot, I can't move...'

'Then don't move.' Marc's voice was still commanding. He was unlacing Felix's boot, easing it off. He set his hand hard against Felix's heel. 'Press. Just a little.'

There was a moan but Felix tried and Ellie thought the moan had been in anticipation of pain rather than pain itself.

'Now the toes,' Marc ordered. 'All the weight's on my hand, Felix, so you won't be moving the leg at all. Just a faint wiggle to let me know you can.'

And Felix gritted his teeth—and wiggled. And Ellie could see them wiggle.

Better and better.

'I need a knife,' Marc snapped and the police commissioner glanced at his watch and groaned with more agony than Felix had displayed. But in unison the bodyguards produced two wicked-looking knives, blades that had been cleverly disguised as cudgels.

And Marc even grinned. 'Let's hope that's the last time these are ever used,' he said and took one and slit Felix's jeans from hip to ankle.

Displaying the whole leg.

'You're sure the braced leg is okay?' he asked Felix, and Felix managed a nod. He was clutching Ellie, sweating with pain and effort.

'When I felt myself fall...I twisted so I'd land on the good leg. But I was trying to hold Mer Noire, 'cos Louis said only the worst horsemen ever let go. And there must have been a rock 'cos it was super hard and it hurt like crazy.'

'I can see that.' Marc was doing a careful examination of the leg, all the way down. Hip. Thigh. Knee. Calf. His strong fingers gently probing.

Ellie watched. This was her role, she thought. She was the doctor.

Not now. The coronation was forgotten. Marc was all doctor.

'It's your ankle,' Marc said and he lifted his hands away so Ellie could see. He'd sliced away Felix's sock. She could see the whole leg now. There was a shallow gash and scrape on his ankle, and the entire area was red and swollen. Marc probed with care while Felix bit his lip and held her hard. He was still a little boy.

And brave.

He was so like his father.

'It might only be sprained.' Marc flashed her a relieved smile, knowing she needed reassurance more than her son. Felix wouldn't have started to think of long-term consequences yet. Marc slit the second trouser leg as well, checking under the brace. Looking relieved. 'Felix, is there anything else? Did you hit your head?'

'No.'

'You're sure?' Ellie was already checking. Never believe a child. In truth, never believe anyone after trauma. The mind did weird things. If Felix's ankle was the major pain then 'minor' trauma could well be overlooked by the neural pathways, meaning lack of pain where pain was needed as a warning. But there was nothing to see. She gave Marc a reassuring nod and she saw him relax.

They'd come out of this so much better than she'd feared. She felt almost sick with relief and she watched Marc's face and knew he felt the same.

'Felix, we're going to have to get you off the mountain,

down to hospital where we can X-ray that ankle and see what's what,' he said. 'But if I had to guess, I'd say there's no fracture. But I bet it hurts. We'll find something to help that now.' He turned to the police commissioner. 'We brought medical supplies—they're back at the junction. Could one of your men…?'

'Go,' the police commissioner barked at his subordinate. Then, almost pleading, 'Sir, the time…if the boy only has a sprained ankle… It's not just the dignitaries I'm thinking of but everyone lining the route, everyone about to turn their television on. We could take over from here. Sir, please…'

Marc looked at her.

He was obviously torn.

But Ellie's mind was clearing. This wasn't the decision he'd made an hour ago—coronation or a son in peril. Nor was it a decision as hard as the one they'd made all those years ago. To walk away from each other.

This might almost be a decision made by parents throughout the world.

My son has sprained his ankle but I'm needed elsewhere. The hospital facilities are adequate. My husband/wife can stay with him.

Need was weighed against need.

Here the decision was obvious and it wasn't heart-rending.

But still Marc gave her the choice. He rose and looked down at Ellie, who was still holding Felix in her arms.

'If you want me to stay I will,' he told her. His gaze met hers and held. 'Nothing's more important to me than you and Felix.'

'Tell him to stay,' Felix said urgently. 'Mum, tell him. I don't want him to be a king.'

'Felix, we don't have a choice.' Her eyes didn't leave Marc's. 'Sometimes there isn't a choice—and there's no choice for your papa now. Your papa is the King, and he needs to accept his crown. The people are waiting. Go, Marc, and go with our love.'

* * *

He rode down the mountain, trying to come to terms with what had just happened. Trying not to think of what he'd left behind.

The medical kit had arrived before he'd left. He'd injected morphine and seen Felix turn from hurting to sleepy. Ellie was staying until the stretcher bearers arrived. They were both safe.

He ached to stay with them but there was truly no need—apart from his desire.

Desire... He wanted them so much it was like a physical hurt. To walk away from Ellie...

To be crowned. To accept a life she'd want no part of.

The police commissioner was barking orders into the phone as they headed down the mountain. 'Notify the Royals at the reception. The parade will start fifteen minutes late. Have the PR people brief the media on what's just happened—no, the boy didn't run away; he obviously went for an early morning ride and his mount got away from him. Brief the security contingent. Let the cathedral know. Have His Highness's clothes at the stables—there'll be no time for niceties.' The orders seemed endless.

Riders were emerging from the forest, men and women in full ceremonial garb who'd been diverted to search for one small boy. There'd be some urgent brushing, removal of twigs, fast grooming of horses, but smiles were everywhere.

The drama was over. Marc could take his proper place.

Except it didn't feel like his proper place.

He knew what he was leaving behind.

They were clattering into the stable yard. The household staff emerged as a fast, efficient team. Brushes, soap and water—this was efficient chaos. The coronation would go on.

As Marc's personal valet, Ernst had time with him. He

looked Marc over with a critical eye. 'There's blood on your shirt. No matter. I have another.' He started helping Marc strip it off. 'Sir, is the boy indeed all right?'

'He is,' Marc said gruffly and Ernst gave him a sharp look. In the midst of the fuss around them, he found time for a little reflection. Maybe he sensed Marc needed it.

'It must have been hard to leave him,' he said thoughtfully. 'His place is with you at the coronation.'

'It can go ahead without him.'

'I know that, sir,' Ernst said gently. 'But, if I may say so, it's a lonely role you're taking on. A man needs his family.'

'I can get by without one.' Ernst was helping him into a fresh shirt, followed by his magnificent coat. 'I have you.'

'Yes, sir, you do,' Ernst said softly. 'And you'll manage the role with skill and with honour. I've served you less than two months and I already know that about you.' He stood back and eyed his handiwork and then tutted as he saw a twig caught in Marc's dark hair. 'But even I have a wife, and I need her.'

'Ernst?'

'Yes, sir?'

'Don't make it harder than it already is.'

The old man's face softened. 'No, sir,' he told him. 'But my heart goes out to you. As, indeed, do the hearts of every person in the country.'

And isn't that the crux of the matter, Marc thought as he finally mounted and readied himself for the parade to begin.

Too many hearts...

I just need one, he said to himself but there was no time for regrets.

The leaders were ready. A slow drumbeat started. The massive gates of the palace were flung open and Dr Marc Falken turned his face to his country.

He turned to become the King.

* * *

X-rays had been taken. The ankle was indeed sprained. Felix would have a few uncomfortable days but there was no drama.

Normally he'd be sent home but, in deference to who he was—and at the insistence of the bodyguards still with them—he was wheeled into a private ward to sleep off the effects of the painkillers.

A ward which just happened to have a television. A large one.

So Ellie watched as Felix slept. She watched the interminable parade. She watched as Marc rode at the head of the vast contingent representing every section of this country.

He wasn't on Mer Noire but on a horse almost as grand, black as night, as regal as its rider.

Marc looked magnificent. There was no other way to describe him.

He also looked regal. Imperious. Breathtaking.

Solitary.

And she thought of his face while he'd searched for Felix. She thought of his agony.

He'd known Felix for barely two months. How could he love him?

And yet that decision made all those years ago was suddenly all around her. That email...

'Do you want your name on his birth certificate?'

And his answer.

'I can't be there for him. I have no right to be his father.'

Adoption had been a decision they'd made together, but blessedly she'd been free to change her mind. Marc, though, had been given no choice.

And now she watched the cheering crowds acclaiming their King, embracing him, taking him as their own, and she knew Marc still had no choice.

But maturity had made her see the cost.

'Felix, you need to wake.'

For the procession had stopped and Marc was entering the cathedral. The trumpets sounded out their triumphant blast. The coronation had begun.

This would be watched in millions of homes throughout the land and recorded a thousand times over. Felix would be able to watch it time and time again. But right now it seemed important—no, it seemed imperative—that they both watched this in real time.

That, wherever they were, Marc knew his family was with him.

As Felix woke and watched, as Ellie held her son and knew that one day he, too, would kneel where Marc was kneeling and have the great crown placed on his head, something settled inside her.

Family.

Once upon a time she'd made the decision to have her baby adopted. She'd changed her mind. Life had been hard in consequence, but she wouldn't give away a moment of what she'd had.

And if she changed her mind about Marc? If she took on a royal role?

There'd be imperatives she'd hate—she knew there would. There'd be moments, days, maybe even years where choices weren't theirs to make.

But what was the alternative?

'He looks like a king now,' Felix breathed as Marc rose, crowned, facing the future, facing his country. 'He doesn't look like my papa.'

'But he is your papa,' Ellie whispered. 'And maybe, maybe, if we had the courage, he could be so much more than just the King.'

The day of the coronation was a day of dignity, pomp and splendour—and reverence.

The pre-coronation ball the night before had held all the pageantry any right-thinking royal could desire. Tomorrow there would be receptions, banquets and a series of lesser balls which Marc would be required to attend, if only briefly. After that, there was a list of regal appointments stretching as far as he dared check his calendar.

For tonight, though, there was a moment of peace. At ten, the dinner for the most important dignitaries was over and Marc was escorted to the chapel.

For this was in his diary as well. Ten to midnight, chapel royal, time set aside for royal reflection.

Actually, Marc hadn't checked his diary this far ahead. He'd been acting on autopilot ever since he'd left Ellie. Oh, he'd demanded updates of Felix's progress through the day. The ankle was indeed sprained, Felix was safely in bed in the hospital and would stay there overnight on the off-chance there were any after-effects. His mother was with him. They were okay.

He'd even been given a message from Ellie herself. *Tell His Majesty that Felix and I watched the coronation with pride. And with love.*

Now, at ten o'clock at night, he was in the chapel staring at his bodyguards.

'Tell me why I'm here.'

'Orders are that you're supposed to be here,' the older of the bodyguards told him.

'It's custom,' Josef said, coming in behind them. 'The coronation programme has stayed the same for hundreds of years. This two hours is scheduled time for reflection.'

'You're kidding.'

Marc stared around at the exquisite palace chapel, the private place of worship for generations of royals, and he thought at another time he might have been glad of this respite.

The silence was almost overwhelming. All day, the shouts of the crowds, the music, the trumpets, the drums, the amassed bands, the noise at the reception, they'd battered him. But here in this place was silence, prescribed, ordered, and he knew what he'd do with it.

'Take me to the hospital,' he ordered.

'Sir!' Josef sounded horrified. 'The agenda…'

'Does it say anywhere that I can't be King if I don't follow the blasted agenda?'

'No, but…'

'But what?'

'The media's gone home,' Josef moaned. 'This is your prescribed quiet time. If you go to the hospital now, the nation will miss it.'

There was a deathly silence, a silence that rebounded over and over from the walls of the ancient place of worship. And, at the look in Marc's eyes, Josef took a step back.

And so did his bodyguard.

'My life is not prescribed by the media,' Marc said, in a voice so low it was almost a whisper. It wasn't a whisper, though. It had the men taking another step back. 'Nor is my life prescribed by any agenda. My life is prescribed by priorities. *My* priorities. My first priority today was my son. Then it was accepting the throne. But now—'

'But if you go to the hospital the media will learn of it.' Josef was still struggling to hold line. 'They'll say the palace held information back.'

'And so it did,' Marc said, and he tugged the great ceremonial sword from its scabbard and handed it to Josef. It had no place in the chapel anyway, and it certainly had no place where he was going. 'But there was no failure. The palace gave the media everything it needed to know about His Majesty, King Marc of Falkenstein. But the King has just decreed he's off duty. Agenda closed. Take the sword, Josef, and put it safely away. I'll take it up again when it's required, but now my need is to be Felix's papa. My need…'

He hesitated, but why not voice what his true need was?

All he could say was what was in his heart.

'My need is to see Ellie.'

* * *

The junior nurse assigned to sit by Felix's bedside was almost asleep. She should have been off duty hours ago but people were celebrating, doing dumb things, and patients kept streaming in.

She'd been due to leave at eight but the nurse manager had pulled her aside.

'I know you're exhausted, but we can't leave the little Prince alone. He's such a high-profile patient. Could you stay for a couple more hours?'

So here she sat, watching a child sleep. A child who'd one day be King.

Who'd have thought? she asked herself. She'd been sad to be rostered to work through the coronation, thinking she'd missed the chance to watch the procession and see real royalty. Yet here she was, watching royalty—although this pale-faced, bruised little boy sleeping soundly didn't seem the least bit royal.

And then the door swung open to reveal…her new King!

He looked at her patient, at the little boy curled up in the big bed, and something in his face seemed to twist. 'Sleeping?'

Somehow she found the courage to reply. 'Y…yes, sir.'

'How is he?'

'Obs all good, sir.' She was struggling to get her voice to work. 'I mean… Your Majesty. Blood pressure ninety on fifty. Temperature normal. He had paracetamol an hour ago when he woke. He also had fruit and custard and asked for his mother, but he wasn't anxious when I told him. It seems he's used to it, sir.'

'So where's his mother?'

'She's…she's in Emergency, sir. When Fe… When His Highness went to sleep someone told her how busy we were and she offered to help. That's why…that's why I'm here.'

And Marc smiled. 'I might have known,' he said. 'Once

a doctor, always a doctor. Thank you for taking care of my son.'

And then he tugged off his beautiful coat, rolled up his sleeves and he turned to the man who'd come in behind him. 'Okay, Josef, let's go do something else the media isn't going to see.'

There'd been no major drama, but the day of celebration meant the emergency department was filled with a seemingly endless stream of minor injuries. Ellie had seen them on the way in.

Felix was shaken and sore, but he was essentially fine. The drugs he'd been given, plus the fact that he'd woken before dawn to creep to the stables before anyone was stirring, had him fast asleep.

Ellie thus had time to herself, and sitting by herself while Felix slept had been doing her head in. After an hour of Felix-watching she asked if she could be fetched if Felix was needed. She headed for Emergency and that was where Marc found her.

She was in the cubicle at the end of the ward. She heard a stir of people arriving and hoped it wasn't yet another drama. She'd had enough for one day, as had the entire staff.

But then the curtain was pushed aside—and it was Marc.

He was back as she'd seen him this morning. Breeches, dress shirt with full sleeves rolled to the elbows, boots...

He was the same Marc and yet different.

This was the King, she thought, and her patient's mother let out a whimper of shock.

'Ellie,' he said and it took a great deal to smile back at him as if he were a colleague.

'Felix...'

'I've just seen Felix,' he told her. 'Fast asleep. I've come to find you.'

'I'm dressing Lisle's leg,' she managed. 'Your... Your

Majesty, this is Lisle Betier, and her mother, Madame Betier. Lisle decided she wanted her dog to watch the Coronation Parade. They have a tiny attic balcony and their dog is big and very old. Lisle's papa is one of your soldiers. He was in the parade. As you can see, Lisle's mama is very pregnant, so Lisle decided to carry the dog upstairs herself. Sadly, she fell. She came in with concussion, but her obs are looking good. I'm fixing her leg now. We can't put plaster on until the swelling goes down but we're bracing it to hold it steady.'

Even though she was telling Marc what was happening, she was also talking to Lisle's mother, doing what she did every day in her medical life. Informing and reassuring. It helped Lisle's mother and it also helped her. It made it almost possible to pretend Marc was nothing more than a colleague.

'Lisle will need to stay in overnight, because of the concussion,' she told Marc. 'But she's going to be fine.'

Marc nodded. He drew the curtains closed behind him, effectively blocking out his entourage, but he too was focused on Lisle and her mother.

'This happened while the parade was taking place?' he asked. 'That was hours ago.'

'You've been…everyone's been busy,' the woman faltered.

'And my dog's been in the car all this time,' Lisle whispered to Marc, as if he alone was responsible. 'By himself. And Mama says we have to worry about me, but I'm sure he's hurt himself. There was blood on his paw.'

'Where's your husband?' Marc asked Madame Betier and she cast him a look that was almost wild.

'He's still on duty. He won't be home until midnight. I didn't even have time to leave a note. I just put Lisle in the car, but she insisted on bringing the dog.'

'He's hurt,' Lisle said stubbornly and Marc lifted an eyebrow at Ellie.

'Has Lisle's leg been treated?'

'It's stable, dressed and braced. Greenstick fracture of the tibula.'

'I want to see my dog,' the little girl whimpered and Marc grinned.

'Well, seeing as your dog—and you—were injured because of my parade, the least I can do is check out your dog. Is he in the car park?'

'Yes.' Lisle's mother was bemused almost to the point of gibbering. 'He split his pad and there was a lot of blood but I did run out and check…'

'But Lisle needs to check too, and this is an imperative.' He tugged back the curtains to reveal Josef and his two shadows. 'Can you find a wheelchair?'

'There isn't one,' someone called from the far side of the ward. 'The nursing home borrowed them to take the oldies to the parade and they haven't returned them yet.'

'There is indeed a lot I'm responsible for.' Marc sighed and looked at Ellie again and smiled. 'But priorities must be maintained. We have an injured dog in the car park, Dr Carson. No other priorities?'

'I don't think so,' she managed.

'Then could you find disinfectant and bandages?' He turned back to Josef. 'I'll need a chair if I'm to work out there, and a decent torch.' He turned back to Madame Betier. 'There have been priorities all day, but maybe this is the last. I, madam, propose to carry your daughter out to the car park. Dr Carson and I will attend to your dog, so Lisle can see for herself that he's fine. While we do that, I'll send word that your husband is to be released from his duties…' he eyed the lady's very pregnant bulge '…for the foreseeable future. On full pay. Starting tonight. Right, team, let's get this priority sorted.'

* * *

Which explained why Ellie was standing in the hospital car park at midnight holding a flashlight while Marc assessed the injured pad of one ancient golden retriever. He treated the dog as he'd treat a child, with all the care in the world, cleaning its split pad, making sure there were no foreign bodies, then carefully padding and binding—and all the time chatting to the dog, to Lisle and to Madame Betier, as if he had nothing more important to do but this.

The bodyguard and Josef were still in the background, but to Marc they might as well not exist. He was totally focused.

He'd been focused all day, Ellie thought. One thing after another...

'There,' he said softly, patting the old dog's head. 'You'll be going home soon.' And then he looked thoughtful. He grinned at Lisle and lifted the old dog out onto the grass verge nearby. He lowered him onto the grass and held him by his collar. The dog didn't put any weight on his injured paw but promptly did what he'd obviously needed to do for hours. And everyone laughed.

Marc took the dog back to the car and then went to pick up Lisle. She needed to be carried back to the ward.

'Marc?'

Ellie's voice made him pause. 'Yes?'

'Could one of your bodyguards carry Lisle back? Lisle, would that be okay? I'm afraid His Majesty has another imperative he needs to deal with.'

'I do?'

'You do,' she told him and took a deep breath because some things were blindingly obvious. Maybe if they'd seen things this clearly ten years ago they would have saved themselves a whole lot of heartache, but sometimes sense took time.

But now...

Sense was all around her. She just needed to shake off his entourage and make Marc see.

They weren't allowed to stay in the car park and talk. That'd be too much for the security contingent to swallow. 'Go back to the palace and have your talk in private,' Josef urged, but some things were too urgent to wait. So Ellie grabbed Marc's hand and led him through the first door marked Staff Only, which happened to be the door through to the scrub room.

No one was there. The row of metal sinks, the bright white lights overhead, the sterile, scrubbed environment, it lent a sense of unreality to what she had to say. And yet it made sense too. She'd met Marc as a doctor. That was what they both were under the trimmings.

And because that was how she felt, stripped bare, in a place where only essentials mattered, she turned and faced him and said the thing that had been pounding in her head for hours. When she'd watched a lone figure take the crown. When she'd seen past the glitz and pageantry to the lone man, solitary, taking on a burden that was surely far too heavy for him to bear alone.

As she'd watched him face what he must face and she'd known she couldn't leave.

'If you still want...' The words had been forming in her head for hours and yet they were still hard to say. But they were the right words. 'If you still want, then I'll stay,' she managed. 'Marc, if you want to make another go of our marriage...'

And there was such a blaze of hope on his face that she took a step back. Almost as if she was afraid.

But then his face stilled. 'Make a sacrifice, you mean?'

And how to explain this?

She was tired, overwrought, overwhelmed by the emotions of the day, yet she still had to get the words out.

'It's no sacrifice. I love you.' The hope flared again but

She held up her hands, as if to fend off any interruption. She had to get this right. 'You know I always have.'

'You know I've loved you. But, Ellie, I have no right...'

'And I thought I had no right either,' she told him. 'Ten years ago we stood in that airport and knew what we were both facing was impossible. We saw no way to be together so we parted. But, Marc, we were married. We loved each other. Surely we could have done it better.'

'Forcing you to join me in a war zone, you mean?' How many times had he thought this? 'And you halfway through your training. With your mother ill.'

'And me? Forcing you to return to Borrawong with me because that was where Mum needed to be? Both were impossible. So we did the only thing that seemed possible. We ended our marriage. But these last few weeks, I've realised... Mark, you can't end a marriage. Sure, a marriage can end if two people fall out of love. If two people should never have married in the first place. A marriage can stop being a marriage, but has ours?'

'What are you saying?'

'I'm saying...' She took a deep breath because she wasn't sure. It should be the guy, she thought, the man who went down on bended knee, but Marc had already done that. He'd already married her in all honour and then he'd walked away because that had been the honourable thing to do too.

He'd asked her to stay now. That had taken courage, she knew, but what had taken more courage was his acceptance of her response. He wanted her. She could see it every time he looked at her. And Felix was his son, and he had a right to be here for him, as he'd had the right these last ten years.

So say it.

'Marc, we haven't been able to be together for most of these last ten years,' she managed. 'And yet...and yet...do you still feel married?'

'You know that I do.'

He was past exhaustion too, she thought. Up at dawn,

riding to search for their son, then going through surely the most demanding, emotionally overwhelming day of his life. He looked almost grey with tiredness. There was a trace of blood running down his sleeve. That'd be from washing the dog, she thought, and she looked up into his tired, careworn face and thought, *Of all days, to be carrying an unknown little girl into the car park and caring for her dog...*

'There'll always be other priorities.' She said it surely now, the sudden remembrance of Marc's tenderness towards Lisle and her dog almost overwhelming her. 'And... and we need to accept that. But if we decide that being married is a given, something that can't be revoked just by getting on a plane, then won't everything else fit in around that? And maybe, maybe we can work on priorities. Not accept them as given. Like your boxes...'

'I don't—'

'Marc, you've been told they're a priority,' she said, urgently now because this was important. This was at the heart of who he was. Yes, he was now Falkenstein's sovereign, and maybe he was also her husband, but part of Marc was also a surgeon. A fine surgeon. He'd told her once he couldn't even remember deciding to be a doctor—he just knew he would be one. So that was a given.

'We can work on this,' she said, urgently now. 'Together. But you need room for your medicine because that's who you are. Tonight you came in here exhausted, and yet fixing a little girl, fixing her dog...it's who you are and I love you for it. And your country has to learn to love you for it too, because they can't ask you to ignore what's part of you. Marc, maybe for now the boxes take precedence, but there's another priority as well, and that's choosing people we trust to share—'

'We?'

'We,' she said, firmly now because this was in her heart. 'If you want me, I won't leave you to face this alone and it

can't be a sacrifice because I love you. Marc, if you'd still like me to stay, to share the burden…'

It was as if the room was suddenly super-powered, pierced by a jolt of something so strong it threatened to blow them both away.

Or blow them together?

She couldn't remember moving. She couldn't remember Marc moving, but suddenly she was in his arms. Her face was somehow thrust upward to meet his and his mouth claimed hers, with all the power of a long line of ancestral kings, with all the power of a man who'd hungered for his wife for ten long years, with all the power of a man who loved her.

How had she ever thought her marriage was ended? She knew as she melted into his arms, as she felt the heat, the strength, the longing, as she felt the absolute knowledge that this was home, that this was priority number one.

Or maybe it wasn't a priority. Maybe it was simply what was.

Ellie and Marc.

If she thought of the future it might well overwhelm her. She didn't want royalty. She didn't want media attention. She didn't want the baggage that would inevitably distract her from her medicine, even from Felix.

But some things were not arguable. She'd fight for what she needed, she thought, but, as Marc's arms held her close, as he lifted her high and swung her, his face ablaze with joy, she thought she'd never need to fight for this.

This was Marc. Her husband.

Hers.

Three months ago Felix had missed out on riding in his father's coronation parade. This parade was just as good. Actually, Felix thought as he rode his beautiful grey mare beside the great golden carriage containing his mother, this might even be better.

A royal wedding.

His mum had been horrified when the idea was first mooted. 'Marc, no. Let's just do it quietly at the council offices.'

'There's no such thing as quiet when you're the King,' Marc had said cheerfully. 'Josef said the coronation did wonders for the economy. How much more so a royal wedding?' He'd smiled, and he and Ellie had shared one of those goofy smiles they did so often, the smiles that Felix was learning to live with—and even like. 'Besides, I'm proud of my wife. We had a registry office wedding once before, if you remember, and we didn't take our vows seriously enough. Let's show the whole nation we mean business.'

So here they were, heading for the cathedral with all the pomp and pageantry the country could possibly crave.

And Felix was on a horse of his choosing. The mare wasn't quite as magnificent as his father's Mer Noire but she galloped like the wind. His leg was good—almost back to normal—and by normal they were saying it'd stop him doing nothing. Which meant when his mum had asked him to be in the carriage with her, there'd been negotiations.

His first idea was to ride behind the carriage in his new car. Or sort of new. For Marc had presented him with an ancient, battered hulk of a 1922 Austin Seven for his birthday. They were doing it up together. Half an hour a day was all Marc could afford, and sometimes there were gaps, so it wasn't nearly ready—for which Ellie seemed profoundly thankful.

'Then I'll ride,' he'd declared. 'I'll be an outrider.'

She and Marc had considered. 'If it's important to you,' Marc had said at last. 'Do it.'

There'd been a bit of that over the last few months. Discussions as to what was important, and what wasn't.

It had seen Ellie sitting up late at night helping Marc sort through interminable boxes, working out priorities.

It had seen Marc insist on a slab of time three days a week, three hospital sessions where he abandoned his royal persona and operated as the surgeon he was.

It had seen Ellie fly out to Borrawong and arrange for locums to become permanent, funded in part by the Royal Household of Falkenstein. 'It seems crazy when there's so much need here,' Ellie had told Marc but Marc had kissed her and hushed her.

'It lets you stay with me without worrying,' he'd told her. 'And that means Falkenstein has a stable government. It's a small price.'

So Ellie, too, was working whenever she could. The hospital was accustomed to the bodyguards now; in fact the junior nurse who'd cared for Felix the night of the coronation was now wearing a diamond, and Ellie's chief bodyguard was never without a great, goofy smile.

More mush, Felix thought, but he grinned as he kept careful pace with the carriage. He couldn't get distracted. He was accompanying his mother to the cathedral to marry his father, and that had to be priority number one.

And then they were there. The trumpets blared forth their *Ode to Joy*. Someone held Felix's horse as he dismounted because he had an even more important role now.

'Who'll accompany you down the aisle? Would you like bridesmaids?' Josef had asked Ellie, and Ellie and Marc and Felix had stared at him as if he was dumb.

'No one else accompanies me but Felix,' Ellie had decreed. 'My son will take me to my husband. On this day of all days, all I need is my family.'

He'd stood in this place three months ago and accepted the crown and he'd never felt so alone in his life.

What a difference three months could make.

What a difference one woman could make.

He stood and watched her walk steadily down the aisle. Josef had suggested full bridal—*the public will love it!*

She'd considered and finally she'd not only given in but she'd actively enjoyed choosing. She was therefore dressed in white, with slivers of crimson netted through her veil and around the trace of the hem of her gorgeous billowing train.

'Because I need a bit of crimson,' she'd told Marc, laughing. 'I've slept in your bed for the past three months, Your Majesty, and me a divorced woman. Scarlet doesn't begin to cut it.'

Her laughter, her candour, her honesty—as well as the work she continued in the hospital—was endearing her to the nation.

And to him. Every day he loved her more.

Felix was walking before her, carrying the ring that'd been back and forth between continents in its quest for its true home.

He'd wear a ring from this day forth too. Some things were imperative.

Dear heaven, she was lovely.

Her dress was exquisite, the antique lace bodice skimming her figure to perfection, the skirt billowing like a cloud, a mass of silken embroidery. She looked young, happy, beautiful.

Felix was wearing the insignia of the Crown Prince of Falkenstein. He looked proud fit to burst.

His wife. His son.

Could he be any happier?

His thought briefly of that appalling morning when he'd learned he'd be King, when he'd thought the life he valued was over. But now he had his medicine. Things were happening in this country that most people had thought would never happen in their lifetime. And he and Ellie, what a team.

He and Ellie.

She was almost to him now. He reached out his hand and she came to him, putting her hand in his. With perfect trust.

She smiled up at him and he thought, *It can't get bet ter than this.*

Who'd want to be King of Falkenstein? No one, he'd thought all those months ago. But now, with this woman by his side...

He smiled at her and then, dammit, he stooped and kissed her because one kiss at the end of the ceremony was never going to cut it.

She smiled mistily up at him. The hand holding his tightened and they turned together to say the vows they already knew by heart.

And, right there and then, the King of Falkenstein decided he was the luckiest man in the world.

The King of Falkenstein had finally sorted his priorities and found his happy ever after.

* * * * *

*If you enjoyed this story, check out these
other great reads from Marion Lennox*

*FALLING FOR HER WOUNDED HERO
A CHILD TO OPEN THEIR HEARTS
SAVING MADDIE'S BABY
STEPPING INTO THE PRINCE'S WORLD*

All available now!

MILLS & BOON®
Hardback – October 2017

ROMANCE

Claimed for the Leonelli Legacy	Lynne Graham
The Italian's Pregnant Prisoner	Maisey Yates
Buying His Bride of Convenience	Michelle Smart
The Tycoon's Marriage Deal	Melanie Milburne
Undone by the Billionaire Duke	Caitlin Crews
His Majesty's Temporary Bride	Annie West
Bound by the Millionaire's Ring	Dani Collins
The Virgin's Shock Baby	Heidi Rice
Whisked Away by Her Sicilian Boss	Rebecca Winters
The Sheikh's Pregnant Bride	Jessica Gilmore
A Proposal from the Italian Count	Lucy Gordon
Claiming His Secret Royal Heir	Nina Milne
Sleigh Ride with the Single Dad	Alison Roberts
A Firefighter in Her Stocking	Janice Lynn
A Christmas Miracle	Amy Andrews
Reunited with Her Surgeon Prince	Marion Lennox
Falling for Her Fake Fiancé	Sue MacKay
The Family She's Longed For	Lucy Clark
Billionaire Boss, Holiday Baby	Janice Maynard
Billionaire's Baby Bind	Katherine Garbera

MILLS & BOON®
Large Print – October 2017

ROMANCE

Sold for the Greek's Heir	Lynne Graham
The Prince's Captive Virgin	Maisey Yates
The Secret Sanchez Heir	Cathy Williams
The Prince's Nine-Month Scandal	Caitlin Crews
Her Sinful Secret	Jane Porter
The Drakon Baby Bargain	Tara Pammi
Xenakis's Convenient Bride	Dani Collins
Her Pregnancy Bombshell	Liz Fielding
Married for His Secret Heir	Jennifer Faye
Behind the Billionaire's Guarded Heart	Leah Ashton
A Marriage Worth Saving	Therese Beharrie

HISTORICAL

The Debutante's Daring Proposal	Annie Burrows
The Convenient Felstone Marriage	Jenni Fletcher
An Unexpected Countess	Laurie Benson
Claiming His Highland Bride	Terri Brisbin
Marrying the Rebellious Miss	Bronwyn Scott

MEDICAL

Their One Night Baby	Carol Marinelli
Forbidden to the Playboy Surgeon	Fiona Lowe
A Mother to Make a Family	Emily Forbes
The Nurse's Baby Secret	Janice Lynn
The Boss Who Stole Her Heart	Jennifer Taylor
Reunited by Their Pregnancy Surprise	Louisa Heaton

MILLS & BOON®
Hardback – November 2017

ROMANCE

The Italian's Christmas Secret	Sharon Kendrick
A Diamond for the Sheikh's Mistress	Abby Green
The Sultan Demands His Heir	Maya Blake
Claiming His Scandalous Love-Child	Julia James
Valdez's Bartered Bride	Rachael Thomas
The Greek's Forbidden Princess	Annie West
Kidnapped for the Tycoon's Baby	Louise Fuller
A Night, A Consequence, A Vow	Angela Bissell
Christmas with Her Millionaire Boss	Barbara Wallace
Snowbound with an Heiress	Jennifer Faye
Newborn Under the Christmas Tree	Sophie Pembroke
His Mistletoe Proposal	Christy McKellen
The Spanish Duke's Holiday Proposal	Robin Gianna
The Rescue Doc's Christmas Miracle	Amalie Berlin
Christmas with Her Daredevil Doc	Kate Hardy
Their Pregnancy Gift	Kate Hardy
A Family Made at Christmas	Scarlet Wilson
Their Mistletoe Baby	Karin Baine
The Texan Takes a Wife	Charlene Sands
Twins for the Billionaire	Sarah M. Anderson

MILLS & BOON®
Large Print – November 2017

ROMANCE

The Pregnant Kavakos Bride	Sharon Kendrick
The Billionaire's Secret Princess	Caitlin Crews
Sicilian's Baby of Shame	Carol Marinelli
The Secret Kept from the Greek	Susan Stephens
A Ring to Secure His Crown	Kim Lawrence
Wedding Night with Her Enemy	Melanie Milburne
Salazar's One-Night Heir	Jennifer Hayward
The Mysterious Italian Houseguest	Scarlet Wilson
Bound to Her Greek Billionaire	Rebecca Winters
Their Baby Surprise	Katrina Cudmore
The Marriage of Inconvenience	Nina Singh

HISTORICAL

Ruined by the Reckless Viscount	Sophia James
Cinderella and the Duke	Janice Preston
A Warriner to Rescue Her	Virginia Heath
Forbidden Night with the Warrior	Michelle Willingham
The Foundling Bride	Helen Dickson

MEDICAL

Mummy, Nurse...Duchess?	Kate Hardy
Falling for the Foster Mum	Karin Baine
The Doctor and the Princess	Scarlet Wilson
Miracle for the Neurosurgeon	Lynne Marshall
English Rose for the Sicilian Doc	Annie Claydon
Engaged to the Doctor Sheikh	Meredith Webber

MILLS & BOON®

Why shop at millsandboon.co.uk?

Each year, thousands of romance readers find their perfect read at millsandboon.co.uk. That's because we're passionate about bringing you the very best romantic fiction. Here are some of the advantages of shopping at www.millsandboon.co.uk:

* **Get new books first**—you'll be able to buy your favourite books one month before they hit the shops

* **Get exclusive discounts**—you'll also be able to buy our specially created monthly collections, with up to 50% off the RRP

* **Find your favourite authors**—latest news, interviews and new releases for all your favourite authors and series on our website, plus ideas for what to try next

* **Join in**—once you've bought your favourite books, don't forget to register with us to rate, review and join in the discussions

Visit **www.millsandboon.co.uk**
for all this and more today!